D1314147

WE ARE MESQUAKIE, WE ARE ONE

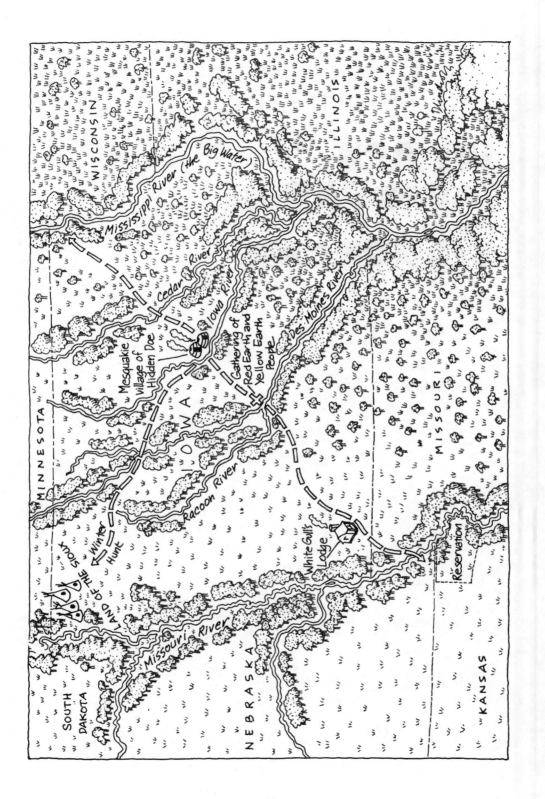

WE ARE MESQUAKIE, WE ARE ONE

BY HADLEY IRWIN

⌐THE FEMINIST
ㄴPRESS

For two wise women—
Pearle and Mary

Library of Congress Cataloging in Publication Data
Irwin, Hadley.
We are Mesquakie, we are one.
   Summary: A young Mesquakie Indian girl grows to adulthood at a time when her
people are forced to move from their home in Iowa to a reservation in Kansas and
encouraged to adopt the white culture.
   [1. Fox Indians—Fiction. 2. Indians of North America—Fiction] I. Title.
PZ7.I712We   [Fic]   80–19000   ISBN 0–912670–85–1   ISBN 0–912670–89–4 pbk.

With special acknowledgment to Judy P. Boyd for her kind assistance.

Production and Design: Anita Steinberg
Art Direction: Susan Trowbridge
Cover Illustration: © 1980 by Marie DeJohn
Map Design: © 1980 by David Lindroth
Composition: Adroit Graphic Composition
Printing and Binding: Bookcrafters, Inc.

ACKNOWLEDGMENTS

WITH THANKS for the help and encouragement of Gretchen Bataille, Chair of American Indian Studies, Iowa State University; Bill Bean, Iowa Department of Public Instruction; and Adeline Wanatee, Mesquakie Settlement, Tama, Iowa.

Of the many resources used in research, particular credit is given to *The Autobiography of a Fox Indian Woman* (1918), a rich source of information on Mesquakie rites, customs, and language patterns.

THE BEGINNING

"GET THE BIRTH HOUSE READY!" shouted Gray Gull.

The Red Earth People were returning to their summer camp. For four suns and four sleeps, they had followed the Big Water south from the winter hunt. Not once had Soft Cloud, big with child, stumbled, though she carried the heavy bearskin of the winter lodge strapped upon her back.

"Put the birth house by the river. For the cleansing," Gray Gull directed.

The older women shed their packs and rushed to the willows while Gray Gull chose the sturdy lodge poles herself.

"They must be strong. Her labor will be hard."

Dogs barked. Children ran along familiar paths leading to the river while the younger women began repairing their summer lodges and digging up the buried bundles of dried food from the autumn before. At the far end of the village, Great Bear, the chief, sat among the braves, just back from the winter hunt, as they told of their kills.

Soft Cloud loosened the leather straps from her shoulders and slumped down. She had told Gray Gull of the pains at midday.

"My daughter, the child must not be born in the fields. It would be a disgrace for you and your husband, Great Bear," Gray Gull warned. "Hurry on."

The pains were coming faster now.

The older women tugged the willow branches into place over the bent lodge poles as Gray Gull snatched up the straps and fastened them at the top of the birth hut.

"Blankets!"

The women brought them to her.

"Now, Soft Cloud," Gray Gull ordered. "Come to the birth hut. Hold to this strap when you feel the pain. I will wait outside."

Gray Gull moved to the edge of the river and sat in the new grass. The River Iowa, swelled by rain, swirled bank high before her.

"Grandmother Earth, you have taught my eyes to see beyond this day, my ears to hear words not yet spoken. I honor the strong medicine flowing from you through me. Care for us and for this girl-child who will be. Teach her your ways so she, too, will be honored among our Red Earth People."

The shadows of the willows touched the far bank of the river. No sound came from the birth hut.

"Gray Gull," a young woman whispered. "One has come from the Yellow Earth People. He speaks with Great Bear."

"He will speak no good. He will talk of White Ones' treaties that force us from our land."

"You have the gift. Your medicine is strong. You see what will be before it is."

Across the village, Great Bear, his face hard like the stone of the river bed, leaned against the trunk of an elm and listened to the messenger.

"White Ones put their feet in the trail of the Mesquakie and Sac. They make our land into fields and gardens. We are told to leave."

Great Bear frowned, his eyes narrow like a tree-cat's at night.

"They are as a drop of raccoon grease falling on a blanket," the One of the Yellow Earth said. "At first we cannot see the grease, but soon it covers the blanket."

Great Bear turned his face to the sky. "This is so. We were once strong. White Ones but a handful of pebbles. Once the land of the Wisconsin was ours. The land of the Big Water ours. Now all is gone. Only the Iowa land is ours."

"Yet they say," the Yellow Earth One went on, "it is written in the treaty we must leave."

"I know no treaty!" Great Bear's hand cut through the air. "Speak no more of a treaty. We stay. Here on our Iowa."

"Bluecoats will come with many horses and guns."

"We stay. We will not fight as our grandfathers did. But we will stay."

Dusk had fallen and the village was quiet as Gray Gull crept into the birth hut.

"How is the pain?"

"I can bear it," Soft Cloud muttered.

"Lie down. When you feel the pain come again, sit on your knees and hold to the strap."

It was midnight. The child had not come.

Gray Gull boiled the herbs and said, "It is all right. You have been wise. You have not eaten of the hazel nut. You did not eat burnt food. You did not lie with Great Bear, your husband. You have carried much wood on your back. The child will come."

She brought a bowl to Soft Cloud. "Sit up. I will hold you while you drink this."

As Soft Cloud drank, Gray Gull sang:

Come out,
You are a girl.
There is no need to hide in fear.
You are a girl.
Come out.

She sang the song four times.

"Now she will be born. Lie down."

At dawn, the child came.

"The way she breaks through the water of birth, her life shall be washed in sorrow and rinsed in joy," Gray Gull proclaimed.

Holding me in her arms, with the trailings of my birth still upon me, she said, "She will be called *Hidden Doe,* and she shall carry the ways of the Red Earth People into many generations."

So Gray Gull, my grandmother, told it to me.

ONE

SHE WAS WADING in Stony Creek the first time I saw her. Her hair, the flaming red of autumn sumac, fell over her shoulders down to her waist. She held up her brown skirt with one hand as she balanced herself with the other and walked among the slippery rocks. Her legs were thin like reeds and white as birchbark. I hid in a clump of willows and watched.

In all my eight summers, I had never seen a White One. Clutching Spotted Fawn, my doll, I huddled deeper among the branches.

I looked all around the banks of the creek, but I could not see the sicknesses and the firewater that Great Bear, my father, said all White Ones bring. All I could see were heavy leather moccasins on the far bank and a headdress made of cloth. She did not seem evil.

With a clam shell, she was pouring water into a crayfish hole and singing a strange song with sounds that ran together like the call of a dove.

"She's no bigger than I," I whispered to Spotted Fawn. "But she is *white.*"

I hugged my doll closer and hunched lower.

"She is playing, Spotted Fawn. See, on the bank. She has made little bowls of mud that dry in the sun."

It was then I heard the loud cry from far down the stream. "Maaay-reeee!"

The white creature stood still; then, like a frightened beaver, she hurried from the water, pulled her headdress over her hair, and carrying her heavy moccasins, disappeared through the long grass.

"Spotted Fawn," I giggled. "That is nothing to fear. She is not evil. She is a *me,* but she is white."

I did not go back to my people at once. I sat among the willows and wondered many things.

For all my eight summers, Gray Gull had warned me to keep watch for "those with pale faces and lying tongues. You will hide, should you see a White One. Hide in the little cave under the roots of the elm that has fallen into the river. Go there by a hidden path. Do not move until I come for you."

I had hidden as my grandmother told me, but the girl was little different from me. I, too, waded in Stony Creek among the crayfish holes and made bowls of mud for Spotted Fawn and set them to dry in the sun. I wondered if I touched the white skin, would it rub off like the limestone along the River Iowa? There were many things I wanted to ask Gray Gull, but I feared she would scold me for wandering so far from our people, and I would be made to fast many days for my badness.

Grandmother Moon was pushing Grandfather Sun from the sky before I returned to our lodge.

Soft Cloud, my mother, was waiting for me. "You have been swimming in the creek with those girls again. I have forbidden you to play with the lazy ones."

"No, my mother. Gray Gull, my grandmother, has taught me if I am to be a medicine woman, I must learn to be alone and not to be afraid. I have been alone and I have not been afraid."

I knew it was a great wrong to lie, but Gray Gull had said, "Hidden Doe is to be a medicine woman as I am." Already I had fasted four suns and been sent out into the darkness, alone, to carry the water from the river.

Gray Gull, my grandmother, appeared at the door of the lodge. "Come and eat. You have strayed far. To-morrow you weed in the fields. I have made the little hoe for you."

For many suns I did not slip off and go swimming with the other girls. For many suns I did not go back to Stony Creek to watch the White One.

For many suns I hoed the green corn. And then the hoeing ceased. I was glad.

"Now, Hidden Doe, you can do this for me," said Gray Gull. "Go to the marshland and bring back the root of the arrowleaf. We have need of this food today."

I left Spotted Fawn on my blanket in the bark lodge, took the basket from Gray Gull, and left the village. I followed the path to the river. I could hear the other girls swimming in the pool of backwater where the river had changed its mind. Laughing Wind called to me, "Hidden Doe. Come swim. We play a new game."

I wanted to join them, for I was the best swimmer, but I wanted more to watch the White One again.

I quickly found the arrowleaf growing in the shallow water. I tucked up my skirts and waded out, wiggling my toes to find the fat roots.

The sun was halfway to its home when the basket

was filled. I hid it in a clump of gooseberry bushes where I knew no muskrat would go. They are our brothers, but they are greedy. The leaves on the highest branches were still and dragonflies hung low over the quiet water as I followed the river down to Stony Creek. I soon left our Mesquakie paths and moved silently through the woods as Gray Gull had taught me. It is something the hunted know. It is something the hunter learns.

The White One was not there. I pushed back the willow branches, and there where I had hidden were two mud bowls, baked hard by the sun. At first I was afraid to touch them. One was tall and had a bent twig looped along its side. The other was flat with blackberries in it, shrunken and dried. The edge of the flat bowl was ringed with thumb prints. It was pretty. I put my thumb in one of the prints. They were the same size. I looked at my thumb. It did not change color. Gray Gull had warned, "Stay away. They would turn you white."

The berries were dry and bitter, but I ate every one.

Still the White One did not come.

I waited. A bluejay scolded from the top of the cottonwood on the far side of the creek. A muskrat swam upstream, and disappeared under water as it neared its home. Willow leaves brushed my face like the fingers of Soft Cloud, my mother.

Then the White One came. I heard her before I saw her. She had not learned to walk like a hunter.

She sat down on the bank and took off her headdress. Then she unstrapped her heavy moccasins and pulled long cloths from her feet. Her skirt was no longer brown. It was orange like the sun as he grows weak in the west. She pulled up her skirt, and she was white even up past her knees.

This day she did not go into the water. She sat in the shade and did not move much. She was very white and under her eyes were strange dark circles as if she were painted ready for the corn-planting dance.

All afternoon she sat, with a flat black board in her lap, marking on it with the soft red stone that my people use to color their faces for battle. Sometimes she would hold up the board and turn it in all directions looking at the crooked lines she had made. Some of the marks were big. Some were little, and she mixed them up.

Again the cry. "Maaaay-ree." She slowly pulled on the moccasins and wrapped her hair in the headdress. She stood for a while, the board clutched under her arm, and looked up and down the creek. She could not see me, but I think she knew I was there.

Again, I was late getting to our lodge, but this time it did not matter. It did not even matter that I had forgotten my basket of arrowleaf roots, for when I got back to our village, my father, Great Bear, led the council, ringed by the lesser chiefs, with Gray Gull, my grandmother, and the other wise and honored women sitting nearby.

Though the women did not speak aloud in council, they talked much and long within the family lodge. The men pretended not to hear, but they listened and heeded the words of the wise women.

No one saw me as I found my mother, Soft Cloud, and sat beside her.

"We will speak later, Hidden Doe, of this day. Tonight, we listen to One of the Yellow Earth."

"We have heard the words of our Sac cousin," my father, Great Bear, was saying. "Words he brings from the White Father in Washington. The words are the same as have filled our ears since before the days of Chief Black Hawk and his wars to save our land. But now we are told there is no place in Iowa land for the Mesquakie, the Red Earth People. We are to be pushed far south of the River of the Missouri. We will talk no more tonight. We will sleep upon our sorrows."

I walked beside my mother to our lodge. Gray Gull, my grandmother, was waiting.

"The arrowleaf?" she said, her eyes like the night owl's.

It *did* matter that I had forgotten the arrowleaf roots.

"You will go. Alone. In the darkness. And bring the roots to me."

I clutched my necklace with its bead of silver that I had worn from the time I was first able to walk and started down the dark river path. Under Grandfather Sun, the steps were few to the marshland, but with Grandmother Moon hidden behind clouds, it was very far, even though I ran until my heart pounded like the drums of our dances.

The next day, Gray Gull said to me, "I will teach you to make reed mats."

It was a long teaching. I made many, many mats until I could make one that satisfied her. I learned to make good reed mats. Then the mat-making ceased. I was glad.

The corn grew high, its tassels pointing to the sky like arrows, before I could get back to watch the White One again.

"You have worked well, Hidden Doe. You have not gone swimming with the lazy ones," Soft Cloud, my mother, told me. "Your reed mats are sturdy. The corn is not yet ready for picking. You may go play with your doll today."

Gray Gull nodded. "She has been good."

I ran into our lodge and got my doll, Spotted Fawn. Gray Gull had made her for me from corn husks, and I had dressed her in beaver skin with moccasins of leather. My mother had painted her face and given her hair from the tail of my brother's pony.

For many suns, as I sat weaving the reed mats, I thought of giving Spotted Fawn to the White One. Mesquakies never take without giving back even more than we have taken.

The White One was not there across the creek from my willow shelter. I waited. She did not come.

I crossed carefully over the slippery rocks to the other side and placed Spotted Fawn against the tree where the White One had sat. Then I went back to my willows to hide and wait.

It was a long wait. I feared she would not come.

She walked very slowly through the long grass and at first she did not see Spotted Fawn. "Cannot eyes of White Ones see the things Mesquakie see?" I wondered.

She lay on her back in the grass. She did not take off her headdress. She did not pull off the heavy moccasins nor the feet cloths. I think she slept. It was when she choked and coughed and turned upon her side that she saw Spotted Fawn.

She stretched her arm toward the doll. The arm was thin as a willow stick, the hand pale as a moth's wing.

"Maaay-ree!" It was the call.

She rose slowly, clasping the doll against her face.

"Maaaay-ree!" The call came.

The White One coughed again, covering her mouth, and when she took her hand away, there was a redness.

She started up the creek toward the voice. She stopped, turned, raised her arm, and waved at me. Then she was gone.

I stayed long among the willows before I got up and walked slowly to my village.

Many times I went back to the willows, but I never saw the White One again.

The corn ripened. The squash yellowed. The feast time came. The days were long and hot. Great Bear, my father, and the braves sat in the coolness of the shade and told of hunts and old victories over the Sioux. Sometimes their voices were low and sad as they talked of leaving the Iowa.

Field work done, the women sat in the shade of their lodges and sewed skins from the winter hunt and watched the children play. My brothers and the other young braves raced ponies across the grassy flatlands. I was much alone. My doll was gone and I dared not ask Gray Gull to make another. The White One came no more to Stony Creek. Even Soft Cloud, my mother, demanded little of me.

And so some days I swam with the other girls.

Heat stilled the day. Laughing Wind called to me as I lingered along the river path gathering firewood.

"Come swim, Hidden Doe. The water is cool. Fish tickle our legs. Come."

I dropped my firewood on the path and ran to the pool, stripping off my skirts. I climbed up on the trunk of a fallen tree and dived. The coolness flowed past my body as I swam underwater and surfaced near the other girls.

We played we were otters sliding down the muddy bank into the water. We swam like trout along the bottom. We splashed like beavers. Nearby, the older girls, shoulder-high in the water, talked of young braves and giggled.

The air grew cool. The older girls left, but we played on. Soon only Laughing Wind and I swam. The woods were still. Laughing Wind hurried from the water and ran into the bushes. Coming down the path was Soft Cloud, my mother. I was left alone on the far side of the pool.

"Hidden Doe," she called, her voice low but firm.

I did not answer. With one kick and a deep breath, I was underwater, swimming like the frightened muskrat for the reeds below the path.

"Hidden Doe," she called again.

I scrambled up the bank, slipped into my clothes, wringing the water from my hair. Quickly I picked up the firewood and started up the path.

"Did you call, my mother?" I asked, with water trickling down the middle of my back.

"We have need of the firewood." She turned and walked ahead of me up the path.

The next morning, I was made to fast and my face was blackened with ashes for punishment.

"You may think we are treating you meanly," my mother said, "but it is because we are fond of you and we wish you to know how to do many things. If we were not fond of you, we would let you play all day with the lazy ones. We do not want you to be that way. We want you to learn to take care of yourself."

Gray Gull said to me, "It is time for you to learn to cook."

So during the hot, busy feast days, I learned to cook: to boil the corn, the potatoes, the beans, the squash, the arrowleaf roots; to prepare the fried bread, the venison, the quail, the hominy; to grind the dried corn for gruel; to gather the wood and carry the water; to scrub the pots and wash the bowls.

I was not hungry during the feast days.

Then came the time of the First Frosty Moon. The corn harvest was over. The winter moccasins ready. The buried bundles of dried roots and corn hidden deep in the land.

Gray Gull, my grandmother, said to me, "Go gather the flowers of the sneezeweed. We will have need of it when the cold of the winter causes the coughing. You will find it on the hills far above Stony Creek."

I left early to hunt the sneezeweed. The oak and maple and sumac had painted themselves red for their battle with the long winter. The Red Earth People move when the spirits of winter come. Trees and grass and bushes are the hair of our Grandmother, the Earth, and must remain. They fight the cold and wind and frost, but they stay until we return.

I passed the willow clump beside Stony Creek, but I did not look across the stream. I pushed waist-high through the long brown prairie grass searching for sneezeweed. I reached the top of the hill. I had never been in this place before. The sky stretched wide above. I looked across the valley. Horses were winding up the hill pulling a wagon with White Ones walking slowly behind.

I turned to find a place to hide. There were no trees, only long grass. Like a snake, I slipped through the grass. I came upon a deep hole with dirt, still damp, piled beside it.

"Someone has gone to Iyapata's lodge," I thought. "Iyapata's lodge lies beyond the sunset and all who die go there."

I could not run. The White Ones would see me. I crawled through the grass and hid many paces from the grave.

The leather on the horses creaked. The White Ones sang a strange chant like the words I had heard on the bank of Stony Creek in the time of the Green Corn.

The horses stopped. I heard a scrape of wood against wood. I raised my head and saw them lift a box and start up the hill toward me.

"An old one must have died," I thought. "They bury on the hilltop."

When I looked again, I saw the box was no bigger than I.

Two men carried the box and behind walked two women. One had hair red as sumac in autumn.

I pressed my face into the grass. I closed my eyes. I clenched my fist against my mouth. I did not move again until I heard the horses and the White Ones leave the hill.

When I returned to our village, I did not cook. The evening meal had ended and the pots and bowls were cleaned.

"Sleep, Hidden Doe," Gray Gull said to me as she sat in the entry of our lodge. "You have walked many paths. Another day we will find the sneezeweed—together."

Two suns came and went before Gray Gull called to me. "It is time, Hidden Doe, to gather the sneezeweed. Soon we must leave for winter camp. Let us go."

Gray Gull led the way along the River Iowa, across Stony Creek, and turned into the valley.

"The sneezeweed grows on the hill," I reminded her.

"There are other things to find today, Hidden Doe," Gray Gull answered as we moved into the woods.

Soon we came upon a worn path leading from the river.

"Why is there a path, Gray Gull?"

"It is a White path."

I looked down. The path was not white. It was red and sandy.

"Who has made this path, my grandmother?"

"They who made it have gone. The earth was not their Grandmother. They tear her hair for fences. They do not share. They know only taking."

I had many other questions, but ahead of us in a clearing stood a lodge of logs such as I had never seen. Gray Gull did not hesitate. She followed the path to the open door, then turned and beckoned me to follow. "I said to you they have gone."

I stood in the doorway. The place for the cooking fire was against a wall, not in the middle. In the other walls were holes for looking out.

Gray Gull, my grandmother, moved about the lodge, her moccasins silent upon the wooden floor. She paused and touched a leather thong that hung upon a peg. She peered into the place for fire and scraped aside the ashes with her foot. She stooped and sorted through dead reeds piled in a corner, then turned to me and said, "Nothing more is here for us. Now we will find the sneezeweed."

We followed the flattened prairie grass where the White Ones' horses had walked across the valley and we climbed to the hilltop where I had grieved for the White One.

Gray Gull sat down beside the fresh grave and motioned for me to join her.

We were silent.

Then Gray Gull said, in a voice more gentle than I had ever heard, "She was your friend. She is still here. It is not yet the fourth day. She has not yet left for Iyapata's lodge."

I wanted to ask how she knew about the White One, but Gray Gull, my grandmother, is a Wise One. She understands all things.

She spoke. "The she-bear always knows where her cub is."

Then I knew I had never been alone while I watched the White One.

"Hidden Doe," she went on, "there are many green things in the woods. Yet the sneezeweed grows where the arrowleaf cannot. You were as two young plants, you of the Red Earth, she of the White. Each must grow in its own place. Each must grow in its own way. It is so."

"Who will guide her to the spirit world? How will she find her way? She was not old. She should not be here on the hill."

"Each in its own way, Hidden Doe. Her way is not yours."

Then from beneath her blanket she drew out Spotted Fawn, the doll I had given to the White One. She placed it in my hands and said, "Now it is time to gather the sneezeweed."

I took Spotted Fawn with me to the winter camp. I never played with her again.

TWO

THAT WINTER we camped far up on the Iowa and moved often, for the hunts were poor. The next winter we spent along the Raccoon and still the game was scarce. Each summer we returned to our lodges on the Iowa.

The next winter my father, Great Bear, said, "We go no more to rivers that flow to the Big Water. We must move on. On to the rivers that run to the Missouri. Only there we find the deer and buffalo."

"There we find the Sioux," my quiet brother said.

"Sioux fly like frightened quail before Red Earth People," my younger brother boasted.

"Puppies bark loudest," Gray Gull grunted. "Many Mesquakie scalps hang on the lodge poles of the Sioux."

My father stood. "I will speak. We must find food. Like prairie fire, the White Ones drive us to hunting grounds of our enemy. We go. We will hunt close beside our lodges. When we sleep, it will be with open eyes."

The walk was long. We camped upon the river of

the Little Sioux. We saw no pointed tipis of our enemies. Gray Gull, Soft Cloud, and I hid our lodge deep in a thicket of scrub oak and bent our lodge poles low. Our mats we wove tightly from reeds, covered them with skins from other hunts, and draped them well with branches.

"When you bring the water, Hidden Doe, do not step upon the same ground twice," Gray Gull warned. "Circle as the fox does to her den. Sioux ride the plains. They know not of the woods."

It was a gentle winter. The hunt was good. My father and my brothers returned. Wild turkeys hung about their necks. The ponies were heavy with deer.

It was a soft day. The snows turned to water, yet winter was not over.

My mother, Soft Cloud, built a fire low outside the lodge, for the day was warm. I helped her and Gray Gull prepare the winter feast. We had long eaten of dried corn and roots. Now we ate of tender venison. We sat on skins to hear the story of the hunt.

"The Sioux," my father said, "are far across the River of the Missouri."

"They hunt only for the buffalo," my quiet brother added.

"Two moons and we can leave the land of the Sioux," my mother murmured. "Our River Iowa waits for us. Our summer lodges wait."

"We cannot stay upon the River Iowa," Great Bear announced. "It is so written in the new treaty. Bluecoats wait for us there."

"It has long been so, yet each time we have returned," Gray Gull said to my mother and sat down beside me.

"I will speak," said Great Bear, my father, and we all listened. "The hungry wolf tracks the wounded bear. The bear can fight the lone wolf. The bear cannot fight the pack. They circle and kill unless the wounded bear flees. We go back to the Iowa to meet our Red Earth People. Then we will go where Bluecoats send us. So it must be. So the treaty says. That is all."

"Soft Cloud, my daughter," Gray Gull began. "I will speak to you of these things," and we all listened. "The wounded bear can hide in its den until the wolves grow weak and seek for other food. If the bear must die, it need not be by jaws of wolves. Our Red Earth People who would follow Bluecoats will forget our ways. They will become as White Ones. We can hide along our River Iowa as the wounded bear in its den. White Ones build their lodges of logs from the forests and cut the earth with their fences. They trample the grasses. They frighten the game and move on. It is so."

"We will hear no more. We will speak again of this. Tonight we feast," my father said.

We ate again. My father and my brothers and the braves fell asleep by the fire, wrapped in their blankets.

As the morning star brightened, Gray Gull woke me. "Breathe of the sneezeweed. You cough and disturb our sleep."

I did as she said and lay down upon my blanket next to my mother.

Gray Gull pulled back the bearskin from the entry. "The fire still burns. It is not wise."

I watched her through the opening of the wickiup as she bent to put out the dying fire. Flames flared up, painting her face with color.

A shadow moved behind my grandmother.

I sat up in my blankets. I thought I dreamed. The shadow crept along the ground toward my father. My grandmother did not see.

The shadow stopped and crouched as if to spring.

I leaped to my feet. "Grandmother! Behind you!"

Gray Gull, blazing log in hand, whirled and struck out in the darkness. A wild shriek broke the night.

My father and my brothers sprang from their blankets, clutching their guns.

"Sioux!" my grandmother shouted and flung the log after the fleeing shadow. Our men raced after him.

"He will not go far. There will be others," Gray Gull warned and shoved me into the lodge.

She snatched up firewood and thrust logs into our hands. "Sioux attack in packs like wolves. Our men are gone. We stand and fight."

Until dawn we did not sleep. Gray Gull stood before our entry, club ready. With the sun, my father and the others returned.

"We chased them across the river. There were but five. They rode swift ponies. We move our camp today."

Gray Gull nodded. "It is wise."

My father and my brothers rested as my grandmother and my mother and I tore down our lodge and buried the ashes of our fires. We left the river of the Little Sioux and built another camp upon a smaller stream.

My father, Great Bear, often told the story of that

night, how *he* and my *brothers* drove away the "twelve" fierce Sioux. Always my grandmother listened quietly with folded hands and smiled, for she knew the truth.

Once, in the first telling, my father spoke of Gray Gull, his voice so low that only I could hear, "Your grandmother is a brave woman."

THREE

THE RETURN to our summer lodges on the Iowa was long. We followed the Raccoon down for three suns to find a crossing, for the river was wide with snow water. The land was green now, with waving grass and patches of white and yellow from the early flowers. Often we walked many steps to keep away from White Ones' lodges that we had not seen on our way to the winter hunt.

Our village was as we left it, lodge poles erect, only bark mats to be mended.

Not always did I work. Not always were the other girls lazy. It was only when they ran from work to swim that my mother called them bad. Many long summer days were ours to talk under the willows, build tiny wickiups, and pretend to be grown up.

One day Laughing Wind and I tired of the other girls and wandered off. We played upon the hill above Stony Creek—the hill where the White One lay. I did not speak of her to Laughing Wind.

The hill was steep. The grass was high. We marked

our starting place, then threw ourselves upon the grass and rolled as far as we could and marked our stopping. Prairie grass clung to our hair and skirts and when we stood to climb the hill again, the sky whirled and our legs could not hold us.

"This will be the last time," Laughing Wind said. "The one who wins decides what we do next. It must be something brave. Something never done before. I have already thought of such a thing."

Laughing Wind climbed to the top of the hill, almost to the White One's grave, and ran, braids streaming out, knees pumping high above the grass. She rolled and rolled and passed my farthest mark.

It was my turn. I climbed even farther up the hill. Where the White One lay, the ground dipped so the grass looked not as tall. I took a big breath, for I must pass the mark of Laughing Wind. I wondered if the White One had ever played such a game, when she was alive. I ran. I ran even faster than Laughing Wind. I flung myself in the grass and rolled far past her mark.

I stood and closed my eyes until the whirling stopped.

"You have won," Laughing Wind said, brushing the grass from her skirt. "What do we do next? It must be something better than mine. I am not going to tell you mine. If I do not like yours, we will do mine, for mine is dangerous."

"For doing mine," I said, for I had thought of it as I stood beside the White One's grave, "we may have to fast for many suns and wear ashes on our faces."

I was not sure that Gray Gull did not watch.

"You think I am not brave? I do not fear the fasting. I carry corn and dried meat so when the fasting comes I do not hunger. See?" Laughing Wind showed me a pouch she hid beneath her skirt.

"Then follow me. No one but me knows of this hidden path."

I led Laughing Wind down the hill, across Stony Creek, and along the River Iowa to where the White Ones' path, now overgrown, cut through the woods.

"I have not been this way before," Laughing Wind spoke, and for once she did not laugh.

"Would you turn back?" I dared her.

"I am not afraid of new ways. But where do we go?"

"We go in ways that no one of our Red Earth People knows. Not even my grandmother, Gray Gull, would put her feet upon this path. Spirits linger there. Ghosts move through the mists at night."

My made-up words frightened even me.

"What will we find?" Laughing Wind followed closer in my steps.

"You will see. First you must close your eyes and hold tightly to my hand. Do not speak. Do not breathe. There may be one who hears."

I led Laughing Wind to the edge of the clearing where the White Ones' lodge stood. Grass grew tall around it. The door, once open, now was closed.

I wished that I had thought of something else to do.

"Now can my eyes open?"

"Only if you dare."

Her hand tightened in mine.

"It is a White Ones' lodge!" Laughing Wind gasped and would have turned to run.

"They who made it have gone," I said. I walked toward the lodge and beckoned her to follow. "Open it."

"Do we dare?" she whispered.

"I have been within," I boasted. "But there is danger. We may turn white. Our people may chase us from the village. We may forever become as ghosts that have no homes."

Laughing Wind giggled. "It could be fun! It would be strange. We could frighten many." She pushed upon the heavy wood. "I will do it!" The leather bands that held the wood creaked and we went in.

All day we played at being White Ones. We fashioned headdresses of locust leaves. We made tall bowls with bent twigs looped along the sides. We made the flat bowl and gathered berries to put in it. We built a fire in the place upon the wall and kept a careful watch, as White Ones do, for Sioux or Red Earth People. We found a flat rock and scratched strange marks upon it with a stone.

"How do you know of these things that White Ones do?" Laughing Wind asked as we lay upon the wooden floor before the fire and chewed on berries from the bowl.

"I have seen many things," I boasted. "I do not always speak of them to everyone."

"Why not? You fear some would tell?"

"I would not care."

"You would care if Gray Gull knew."

Already I could feel the ashes on my face.

"You must not tell!" I cried. "I would not speak about the pouch that saves you from the fasting."

Laughing Wind propped herself up on an elbow and looked into my eyes. "We must never tell!"

"We must make a vow," I said.

Laughing Wind sat up on her knees. "Yes. A vow. It should be dangerous. What should we do?"

"We could make a mark from the White Ones' fire upon our wrists."

"But that would hurt."

"Danger always hurts. The mark would stay forever. We could see it always and remember."

"Yes, remember not to tell," Laughing Wind agreed.

Not thinking of the pain, I grabbed a burning splinter from the fire. I pressed it to my wrist. Laughing Wind held out her arm. I did the same to her.

"Now we are sisters to the end," I said and flung the splinter back into the fire.

"And you will not tell about the pouch?"

"I will not tell. Nor will you speak to Gray Gull of this place."

Many times Laughing Wind and I played in the lodge of the White Ones. If Gray Gull knew, she did not speak of it.

Then it was time for us to work again.

I sat with Gray Gull weaving the mats. My face felt warm and my back ached. I could barely make my fingers move.

"Twelve summers ago we hurried to make the birth hut for your mother," Gray Gull said as her fingers flew through the reeds.

I nodded as she told me again the story of my coming to the Red Earth People.

"We will make small mats. The time is now for you to become a woman. We must prepare the little wickiup."

"I do not understand, Grandmother."

"The time has come when you must watch yourself. You are nearly a young woman. Today we build your own lodge. It must be far from the village. It is not right to be near men nor to stay in the big lodge when the bleeding comes. I will be with you. I will teach you how to be a woman. I cannot tell you why it is. You will know when it comes."

"Will it be as long as the fast days?"

"It will be longer. It will be different. Mesquakies fast for many reasons. When you were a child, it was your punishment. Now it is a step in your becoming a woman. At other times, it is to help us bear the sorrow when those we love die."

"Will I be afraid as when you sent me alone in the dark for water?"

"Yes. But only the first time."

Far from our village, hidden in a clump of thick hickory bushes, I built the wickiup. As I worked, I felt the bleeding. I lay down on the forest floor. I cried, for I was afraid. Soft Cloud, my mother, found me.

"Stop crying. It is the way with us women. We are made to be this way. Nothing will happen to you."

My mother led me to the little lodge I had built. "Go inside and stay. Gray Gull will come to you."

Gray Gull came. "You will pound the corn into hominy. You will eat only of this for ten suns."

Together Gray Gull and I lived in the little lodge, and she told me of many things. She told me of the Red

Earth People and how we came to be. She told me of
seeds and how they grow. She told me of the plants I
would use for healing when I became a medicine
woman. She told me how to be a woman.

"I seek the good life," Gray Gull spoke. "I have
reached an old age. You must do the same. A Mesquakie
woman lives thoughtfully and proudly. Her voice is
heard, though not in council; still she is honored and
heeded. The lodge and everything in it are hers. The
fields are hers. She plants and harvests. A Mesquakie
man lives proudly too. Ponies and weapons are his. He
hunts and fights. Together we are strong. Together we
are equal. Together we are Mesquakie."

"What must *I* do to be a woman?" I asked.

"Understand that men will now desire you. A Mesquakie woman walks quietly and proudly on her own
path. She does not laugh and talk with every man who
desires her. She chooses wisely the one who honors her.
And there is more."

I was very tired and would have slept.

"Treat all old people well. Do not lie. Do not steal.
Do not be cross. Be kind to all. Share the things you
make. That, my grandchild, is the way of the Mesquakie
people."

Time was long. No one came to me except Gray
Gull, my grandmother. Each day she instructed me in
the Mesquakie way. Each night she slept beside me.

On the morning of the tenth sun she said, "Take off
the soiled clothes you wear. Wrap them in this deerskin
bag and hang the bag on the tree behind your lodge."

I did as she directed.

"Now," she said, as I stood before her naked, "Go
bathe in the river until you are clean."

The water was cold, but I swam until my skin was smooth as the catfish, and I would have run through the woods like ponies when they have shed their straps, had not Gray Gull called to me, "Here are your new clothes. I have made them for you. Put them on, for now we build your next lodge beside Stony Creek."

"Why must this be?"

"Every Mesquakie woman, at her first bleeding, stays ten suns in each of two places, far from the village. The bleeding will come as Grandmother Moon wills. After this first, you will need but one little hut, and your time will not be as long."

Ten more suns, Gray Gull and I lived together in the lodge by Stony Creek. Still I ate but of the hominy. Now she came to me only at night.

"When I am gone, think on the things of which I speak. Consider the one who is called Hidden Doe. Listen to the leaves as they talk to each other. Watch the turtle dove as she builds her nest. Learn how the beaver cares for its young. Think upon hidden paths and learn to follow them."

I thought of many things as I sat beside Stony Creek throughout the ten suns. I thought of the White One on the hill, of waters running to the Iowa, of leaves dying in the snow, of my Grandfather Sun who never dies. I looked long into the waters of Stony Creek at Hidden Doe.

At the end of that time, Gray Gull came to me and said, "Go bathe in the creek. Prepare yourself for the feasting and come to me clean."

I did as she told me and walked alone back to our village. No one looked at me, yet Gray Gull had said, "Now you are a woman."

The men sat before the fire. Gray Gull took my hand and led me into the circle of women. "Speak to this one," she said, "for this is Hidden Doe who has fasted many suns. She is a woman."

Each woman came to me and set a gift before me.

Then Gray Gull said, "Now, Hidden Doe, to show this change in you, take the food and give it to the men as your mother does."

I was a Mesquakie woman.

FOUR

Now THAT I had waited and fasted through the twenty suns, I was no longer a child. Without being told, I hoed the green corn. I sewed the winter skins. I gathered the roots for medicine. I cooked the dried venison. I walked proudly in old paths.

The corn was harvested. The feasts were over The dances done. Seeds for the planting were stored in the earth. We were ready to leave our summer village again.

Gray Gull helped me roll and strap the heavy bearskin to my back as we prepared for the long way ahead. This year we would go to different hunting ground where there was little chance of meeting Sioux warriors and where the smoke from the White Ones' lodges did not smudge the sky.

My father, Great Bear, and the other braves waited with their ponies at the far side of the village beyond the trees where our fields began.

I remembered then that I had left Spotted Fawn, my doll, under the sleeping platform of our bark house. Although I no longer played with her, I sometimes, at night, held her inside my blanket and thought of the White One.

I turned to go back to the lodge for my doll, but Gray Gull clutched my arm.

"Listen! They come!"

I heard nothing but the shouts of the children and the barking of our dogs.

"Who comes?" I asked, but Gray Gull ran forward, calling to the women.

"They come! They come!"

They rode up from the river, their blue coats black against the colors of autumn, their guns glistening in the morning sun. They trotted past me. I was frightened. The horses were big and the men's faces white where the hair did not grow. They did not look at Gray Gull nor me nor the rest of the women, but rode on in a swirl of dust up to my father.

One from the Yellow Earth was with them and he talked to my father, repeating the words that the Blue-coat told him. My father stood beside his pony until they were through speaking; then he motioned with his hand the direction we would go for the winter hunt. Bluecoats moved their horses in closer. The One from the Yellow Earth spoke more words and pointed back toward our village. My father shook his head.

I crept up beside Gray Gull. "What is happening?"

"I think they are telling us we must leave and never come back." Her voice was harsh and her eyes looked over our village as if she were not seeing.

"What will we do?"

"We will wait until your father speaks. It shall be as

the council decides. As always we will go on the winter hunt and return here for the planting."

Bluecoats talked long with my father. The women sat on the ground, their packs still strapped to their shoulders. I was glad to sit.

The circle of Bluecoats opened, and my father mounted his pony and rode toward us. He said to Gray Gull, "We leave in peace for the winter hunt. We cannot return to this village."

"We will leave for the winter hunt," Gray Gull agreed. "We will speak of the other later."

My father turned and rode past the Bluecoats, and the other braves followed. We stood and walked silently after them.

We were far out on the open prairie when Gray Gull turned to look back toward our village.

"They burn . . . our . . . lodges."

Threads of gray smoke rose and mingled in a dark cloud that veiled the sky above our river.

A moan came from our women.

"What do we do?" my mother asked.

"We go back!" announced Gray Gull. "Though they burn our lodges, they cannot burn the earth."

I thought of Spotted Fawn hidden beneath the platform of the bark lodge, and I blinked so I would not cry.

As one, the women turned and walked back toward our river.

We camped that night among the willows along Stony Creek. We did not go to our village. One of the braves said, "Everything is gone. Even the earth is scorched "

That night the council was long. Many spoke. I sat in the circle of women and listened until I fell asleep.

My father's voice woke me. "We cannot agree. We will speak of this again."

We left for our family fires. Gray Gull stirred the ashes and added more wood. The talk continued, my father speaking only to my uncles and my brothers, Gray Gull speaking only to my mother and my aunts, but all listened. It was the Mesquakie way.

"We can go on our winter hunt. We cannot return to this village. It is written in the treaty. Already the others have gone: Keokuk, Poweshiek, Hard Fish . . . all lead their people toward the west. Black Hawk, the great leader, is in chains." So spoke my father.

"Treaties are but milkweed blown on the wind." So spoke Gray Gull. "Our Grandmother Earth knows no treaties. The land does not belong to us. We belong to the land. One cannot trade what one does not own. We stay on our river. Should we leave for the winter hunt we are saying we no longer care. We say, 'Come, White Ones. Come take our land.' We stay here and remain Red Earth People. We go, and the Mesquakie will be no more."

It was decided. We would not leave our Iowa. We would scatter along the river like quail when they hide their nests in deep grasses. In the spring we would gather to plant our fields again.

I did not go back to our village to search for Spotted Fawn. I did not go near the spot where I had found the bowls baked in the sun. I did not climb the hill where the White One lay.

We built our winter wickiup far from all others and stretched the bearskin over the doorway. It was a sad time, but I was glad I was not walking the long way to the winter hunt carrying the heavy bearskin.

My father and my uncle and my brothers left to hunt alone. It was not like before when all the men of the village rode off together, whooping and shouting and boasting of the kills they would make.

"They will be back before the snow," I said to Gray Gull as she shaded her eyes against the noon sun and watched them ride away.

"Though you are a woman, you speak as a child. They will ride many moons to find the deer. Deep snows will come before they return. The winter will be hard. The woolly caterpillar wears a heavy coat. Already the leaves drop from their mother tree and the wind moves to the north."

All this was true. The winter came early. I gathered the roots until the ground was frozen. We did not eat of the corn from our packs, but saved it for the return of the hunters. I broke the ice and caught the fish, and we ate. We did not relish it. Gray Gull dipped up the food and there was never enough. Often my mother did not eat her portion, but scraped it back into the pot for the others.

Soft Cloud and my aunt and I gathered wood from the fallen branches along the river. Gray Gull cared for our meager fire. When the wind swept down the ravine, our wickiup filled with smoke, and I coughed until my throat burned and my eyes watered. Some days I feared the redness that I had seen on the White One's hand.

The snow fell deep around us, and still my father and the others did not return.

I sipped the gruel of corn and melted snow.

"My father and my brothers eat venison tonight," I said to my mother. "Had we followed them on the hunt, we too would eat."

"It is as it must be," my mother answered.

"I am cold. The fire is thin," I complained.

"Go then and gather more wood," Gray Gull said.

"My father would have us go with Bluecoats to the south. It would be warm." I said this to my mother, but I looked at my grandmother.

"You chatter like a winter squirrel," my mother whispered.

"The North Wind beats at our wickiup. He covers it with snow. The log lodge of the White One stands empty across the frozen river."

"My grandchild. I take pity upon you. I am much grieved at your wailing and weeping. Red Earth People do not walk in the ways of White Ones. We do not eat of their food. We do not drink from their bottles. We do not dress in their clothes. How then would you have us live in their lodge? Would you have us turn white?"

"We would not starve. We would not freeze," I said, clutching my blanket about me.

"Your father and your uncle and your brothers are far in the northern lands searching for our food. Their dangers are greater than ours. Are you so much less than they?"

I stood up and went out into the winter storm to gather more firewood, but I could not understand how living in the White One's lodge could change me.

We were deep into the winter. The snow stopped. The wind grew still. The ice on the river cracked like my father's gun. We sat close to the fire, our blankets wrapped tightly around us. My mother grew thin and ill. Some mornings she did not rise to join us, but lay with her back to the fire and was silent.

Bright Feather, Grandmother's friend, pulled aside the bearskin one morning and stood before us.

"Come to our fire," Gray Gull spoke. "You have walked far in this bitter cold."

Bright Feather sat down and pulled a bundle from under her blanket. "We starve," she said. "Many have died. The very young. The very old. Our ponies, too. We have begged of the White Ones whose lodges surround us to the south. I bring you their food."

She held out the bundle.

I watched my grandmother, Gray Gull, take the gift and nod. "The winter has been hard and long. But soon our men return from the hunt and we plant our fields again. Hidden Doe, bring me the corn. We will share our food with Bright Feather as she has shared with us."

I knew it was the last of our corn.

Bright Feather stayed the night and left in the winter dawn. I waited for Gray Gull to open the bundle. For a long time she sat and stared into the fire. Then she stood up, took the bundle, and opened it. It was bread! White bread with golden top!

Slowly she tore the bread into pieces and flung them into the fire. My mother did not see. My aunt turned her face away.

I watched the bread shrivel and become ash. Bitter

smoke filled the wickiup. I covered my head with my blanket and cried in hunger.

"We may starve. We do not beg," my grandmother said and sat down before the fire and said no more the rest of the day.

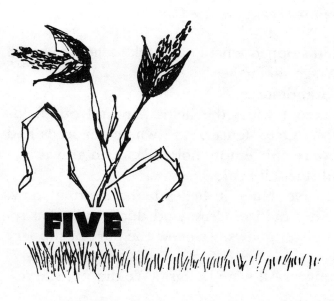

FIVE

My FATHER and my uncle and my brothers returned, but they brought little game. The rabbit was thin and tough. We chewed the scanty meat and broke the bones and sucked the marrow. It was then Gray Gull said, "We will go to our village and dig up the seeds we have left for spring planting. We must eat our seeds to live."

The day was heavy and dull; the wind was cold. Ice was beginning to melt on the creek, and the path to our village was slippery with mud.

"What will we plant, if we eat our seeds?" I asked, as I followed in Gray Gull's footsteps.

"There will be no planting. We will live as our Old Ones did. Our Grandmother Earth will provide."

"I smell the smoke of the burning, Grandmother," I said.

Gray Gull did not answer.

We walked through our village. Only a few charred lodge poles, black and broken, showed above the snow.

Gray Gull stopped where our bark lodge had stood and said, "We go no farther."

"Why, Grandmother?"

She pointed toward the fields. Around our fields stood the White Ones' fences. And where our seeds had been buried were only empty holes like open graves.

"We will starve," I said.

"We will live. Nuts lie beneath the melting snow. Fish move under the ice. Geese and ducks will soon return. When hunger gnaws, we chew the bark of slippery elm."

I was hungry. All were hungry. We did not starve.

With the coming of spring my brothers were sent to call our people back for council. We could not gather at our village. Instead we met in the valley below the hill where the White One was buried. We were fewer than before. We did not build our bark lodges. We spread our blankets on the earth and slept beneath our Grandmother Moon.

We lived on small game and ate of the berries before they were red. Many grew sick, but no one died. My mother, Soft Cloud, grew stronger, for I gathered teal eggs and mixed them with herbs as my grandmother had taught me.

The council fires burned long through many suns and sleeps. We lived like lost and homeless people. We feared the Great Spirit was hidden from us. My father, Great Bear, spoke long at the council of the land promised us. Of flowing rivers and wooded hills and rich earth ready for the planting in the Kansas Land far to the south, of Bluecoats waiting to feed us and give us seed for the planting in the new land, of deer and antelope and buffalo which we had not seen by our River Iowa for many seasons, of land where neither Sioux nor White would threaten.

And so it was decided.

Gray Gull sat in the circle of the Honored Ones as if she neither saw nor heard.

Then Roaring Thunder, my uncle, spoke—my uncle who had not spoken in the council before. "You must go to the Kansas Land. You must go to live. Some of us must stay here so our old ways can live. Our Red Earth People who would follow Bluecoats will forget Mesquakie ways and become as White Ones. Those of us who stay will hide along the Iowa as the wounded bear in its den. We will find a way. We will watch and wait for your return."

Gray Gull nodded. They were *her* words. I knew them well.

My father, Great Bear, said, "So it shall be."

I sat in the outer circle of the women and said to my mother, Soft Cloud, "I will stay with my grandmother and find a way."

When the Bluecoats came, I sought out Gray Gull and said, "I would stay with you, my grandmother."

"Do not entreat me to let you stay," she said and turned away from me. I could not see her face.

"Where you stay, I would stay. Where you die, I would die."

Gray Gull walked away from me toward the river. I followed her. I could speak no more words.

"Go, my granddaughter. Go and carry the old ways with you. Our people will have need of them. You will return. And though I die, I will be here waiting for you."

I went from her and joined my father, Great Bear, and my mother, Soft Cloud. I strapped the bearskin to my shoulders. When I turned to look, Gray Gull, my grandmother, was gone.

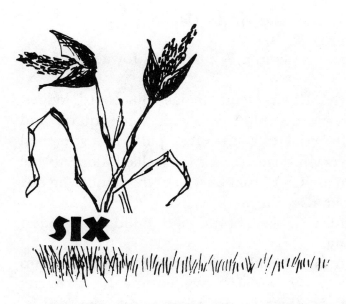

SIX

"WE GO only beyond the Red Rocks," Great Bear, my father, said when we grew weary of the walking and sick at heart for our River Iowa. "On the waters called by White Ones 'Demoine,' we wait."

"For what do we wait?" I asked my mother.

"For all Red Earth People. For all Yellow Earth People. When all have come, Bluecoats take us to the Kansas reservation."

We would have lingered along the lazy streams, but Bluecoats were never far from us and White Ones' lodges blackened the land.

"Will we plant seed by the Demoine?" I asked.

"No Iowa land remains for us. We will use the White Ones' food. Our men will hunt," my mother said as we crossed the river.

They put us on a land where grass was flat and brown from many steppings. Never had I seen such a gathering of people, like the swarming of bees. Voices drowned the sounds of leaves and calling birds. I was

45

alone with my people in a White Ones' Iowa, and I was frightened.

Across the River Demoine lay Bluecoats' lodges, thick and heavy as boulders. Fields were square and fenced and slashed with White Ones' paths that stretched across the river on dead oak logs. I walked alone to the edge of the river. There I sat and wept, remembering our village and our River Iowa.

I helped my mother, Soft Cloud, build our wickiup for the waiting.

I walked far to find wood for our fire. I came up from the river, the wood heavy on my back. Many young braves on their ponies raced across the prairie. The pounding of hooves made the earth shake. My boasting brother was among them, and I stopped to watch as he galloped past, his body flat against his pony's neck.

It was then I heard the young brave. He was of the Yellow Earth. He spoke to the others in a laughing voice. He spoke of me.

"The Red Earth One is small for such a heavy load. She gathers the good wood. She will be a fine wife for a brave warrior."

I felt the others turn to look at me.

"Her legs are strong," said another.

I did not look. I did not laugh. I walked away.

"She did not see you, Black Crow. She heard your cawing. She did not look."

Their shouts and laughter followed me as I hurried back to my mother. When I was far from them, I turned to see the one they called Black Crow. All the others looked now at the ponies, but he still looked after me.

He was tall and straight as an elm lodge pole. His shoulders broad and strong, like my brothers'. Upon his head he wore a White One's hat.

I hurried to build the fire. I did not speak of this to my mother. Still I heard his voice and saw the White One's hat.

My father and my quiet brother went alone upon the hunt. My boasting brother, racing his pony with Black Crow and the others, shouted, "I will follow later when you find the game."

The wild turkey had flown far from the big river, the deer fled before Bluecoats, and the buffalo hid in the land of the Sioux.

Returning without game, my father brought from the Bluecoats strange foods. We learned the White Ones' words: "coffee," "tea," "bacon," "flour." I ate, but thought often of Gray Gull. My father did not hunt again. He sat among the others and talked of past hunts.

The time of the green corn came. There was no corn. The time of ripening came. There was no harvest. We women resewed old skins. We sat in the shade making beadwork. I fashioned a butterfly, bright as the ones that darted through the green corn of our Iowa along the river, and wove it upon a band for the dancing.

Though we were often sad, we danced.

The moon of the harvest was at its fullest. The drums sounded. The rattles shook. The dance began. Soft Cloud, my mother, and I stood. Her eyes closed as she listened to the pounding feet of the braves. Her moccasins moved in time to the beat. She left to join the circle of women and match their stately step.

I stood alone.

"You do not join the dance as your friend, Laughing Wind, does." I knew his voice. I did not turn to seek Black Crow's face. "You do well not to look at boasting braves."

I watched my mother in the circle of the dance.

"You are a quiet one. You do not laugh."

I did not turn my head. I moved my eyes, but could not see him. He stood behind me.

"You only carry wood?"

I wanted to smile. Then I wanted to turn upon him and shout, "I carry the bearskin on the winter hunts!" Instead I stepped closer to the circle.

"You are an old woman. Learn new ways."

Then he was gone. I saw him join the young braves behind the trees and tip his head back to drink long from a White One's bottle. He still wore the White One's hat.

The Red Earth People did not dance again on Iowa Land.

"The Rutting Moon has come. Bluecoats take us now to Kansas Land," my father said. "We leave upon the night of the Full Moon."

We sat upon the banks of the Demoine that autumn night and Great Bear spoke: "In the sky, the bear runs and the three hunters follow."

I looked up at the stars. I knew the words well.

"From winter through summer, the hunters follow the bear. Now they catch and slay it. See how its blood covers the trees and turns them red. But the bear will come to life again. The hunting will begin again. Even though the bear is slain, he will come back to life. It is so."

No one rose to speak. Words dried in our throats. Even Laughing Wind, who sat by me, was quiet.

Across the Demoine, brighter than the moon, shone the torches of the White Ones, as many as the stars.

"Why do the White Ones' fires dance so wildly?" I asked my mother.

At first she did not answer. Then she spoke. "They wait to take our land. With the firing of the big gun, the land is theirs. The treaty says."

It was so.

The cannon sounded. It echoed through the valley like thunder after lightning's arrows. The torches of the White Ones rushed toward us like prairie fire. The river did not stop them.

My father rose and said, "We go."

We left Iowa and followed the Bluecoats as the white settlers staked their claims upon our land.

SEVEN

The Kansas Land was not the land of promise.

Great Bear, my father, had said, ". . . a land with flowing rivers and wooded hills and rich earth ready for the planting."

"Great Bear. This will be your field." White Agent led us far from our lodges, across the flat prairie, to a patch marked off by split log fences. The hot sand burned my feet as I followed my father and mother and aunt.

"I am a hunter." My father frowned. "I am a warrior. A chief. It is the women who plant and harvest."

"You must change your ways, Great Bear. You are on the reservation. You have no need for warriors. No reason to hunt. You can buy the food you eat with the money we will give you."

"You do not *give* us money. You *pay* us because you have taken the land."

White Agent shook his head and scuffed his leather boot in the sand.

"Now, Great Bear. You'll have to do things differently here than you did back on the Iowa."

My father turned and walked back to the village.

White Agent dropped the bag of seed at our feet. The kernels of corn were pale and white as if bleached long in the sun. I searched for the bright colored kernels of our corn, but all were white as the bread my grandmother had thrown in the fire that terrible winter.

Across the fence, Bright Feather, my grandmother's friend, scratched in the sand with her hoe. I looked beyond her. All the other women of our village hoed and planted in their own little squares.

"We will tear down the White Ones' fences that separate us, my mother," I said. "We will have but one field and one fence around us."

Soft Cloud turned her head slowly; her eyes followed the line of fences that divided us. She nodded and said, "They pen us like their animals. Their fences will make good firewood."

Together we Red Earth Women tore down the fences and spent the day carrying the good wood to our lodges. The next day we prepared the large field together.

White Agent came. He did not smile. He did not build any more fences to divide us.

The corn grew frail and yellow from the White Ones' seeds. I hoed in the field with our women. Often I hoed alone, for I was sick at heart for our good land.

Sand pebbles stung my face as he jerked his pony to a stop beside me. It was the one called Black Crow.

"Here is the old woman again. Can she talk yet?"

He wore the White One's hat. He wore the White One's shirt of green as bright as growing corn.

I chopped at the weeds and moved down the row. He followed me on his pony.

"Why do you come to the fields? Are you a woman?" I said to him, without raising my head from my work.

"Why do you not look at me and see I am a man?"

I wanted to giggle, for I knew he was a man. I feared my mother would see us in the field. I did not laugh, but I looked up at him.

He moved his pony forward. "Tonight the Shawnee show us a new dance. It is called the Snake Dance. I will be there."

I pointed to his shirt and hat and said, "You are a White One. How can a White One learn a Shawnee dance?"

He laughed loudly and shook his head. "You are still an old woman. But at least you talk."

He turned and rode away, and it was good, for soon my mother came to hoe in the field.

As we worked, I asked, "Do you know of the Shawnee Snake Dance?"

My mother stopped hoeing and her voice was sharp. "Where have you heard of such?"

"I heard the others talking as I hoed. It is tonight they dance."

"It is no dance for good women. Were you to go, you would disgrace your family. It is for those who are free and wild and follow the White Ones' ways."

I did not see the Shawnee Snake Dance. I sat in the doorway of our lodge and listened to the drums and for Black Crow's shouts.

Soon the time came for Great Bear to lead our Red Earth People to White Agent's house to receive the money promised us. I saw the others going in long lines past our lodge—Sac, Ottawa, Chippewa.

"Why do the Red Earth People not go to White Agent for our money?" my boasting brother asked. "Soon we leave for the hunt and will need guns and food."

My father sat in the doorway of our lodge, his back straight, his eyes dark with anger.

"Red Earth People do not beg. Let those who took our land *bring* the money to us."

"But if they will not bring the money, what then? I have need of my share," my brother said.

"I know for what you need your share. For White Ones' bottles. You would be like your friend, Black Crow, who spends his days drinking and gambling and speaking loudly with some of the women."

I sat beside my father and dared not move.

"I am your son. I have a right to my share." My brother's voice was blurred and loud. My boasting brother was as a strange one to me.

My father stood. "I speak no more with you. We wait for White Agent to come to Great Bear."

The corn ripened ready for the harvest. I rose early and walked alone to the field.

The corn was trampled and broken, and ponies milled among the stalks tearing at the corn ears. Many ponies. Black Crow's pony. My boasting brother's pony. The log fence lay splintered and broken where they had come through.

I ran down to drive them from the corn. Then I saw

my brother and the others and Black Crow sprawled on their backs in the field.

"They are dead," I cried. Then one of them snored loudly, coughed, and went back to sleep. I shook my brother's arm but he would not wake.

I ran to get the women of our village.

Like swooping hawks, we drove the ponies out. My brother and the others did not stir.

"And what of the drunken ones who sleep in our field?" Bright Feather, my grandmother's friend, asked. "They have been drinking White Ones' whiskey."

"These young warriors grow bad in this new place. Soon they leave for the hunt and become men again." My mother turned and we followed her out of the field.

No, the Kansas Land was not the promised land.

Great Bear, my father, had said, ". . . a land of deer and antelope and buffalo."

My father and my brothers and the other Red Earth warriors left soon to hunt the buffalo far away on the Great Plains. I closed my eyes and listened to their shouts and boasts. It was as it had been upon our Iowa.

While the men were gone, one came from the Iowa Land with words from my grandmother.

We sat in our lodge around our fire with the old men of the village and listened.

"These are the words Gray Gull told me to speak," he began. " 'We live beside the Iowa. The long hunts are no more. Woods shelter us from Bluecoats. Smoke from White Ones' cabins fills the sky. They do not see us. We do not beg. We eat small game, wild plum, nuts and berries. We live.' "

I saw her. My grandmother, Gray Gull. The soft

wrinkles, the flashing eyes, the firm mouth, her unbent body. I heard her voice, deep and strong, and it spoke to me.

" 'I sit often alone on a hill above Stony Creek. I think of many things. I consider White Ones' ways. I think on Mesquakie ways. I learn. I seek a way. That is all.' And so Gray Gull instructed me to speak."

Through many sleeps I thought on Gray Gull and the things she had taught me.

The hunters returned with the first melting snow. I saw them far out on the prairie. They rode slowly as if burdened with game. I called to the village, "They come."

Children ran out to meet them. I waited with my mother by our lodge.

The deer were small and thin. The buffalo few and old. My boasting brother dead.

At the council, Great Bear, my father, told of the hunt. "For thirty suns we crossed the plains before we found the buffalo. Cheyenne and Comanche met us in battle. We slew many and drove them away. They slew my son, the boasting one. We hunt no more upon the Plains."

The next day my father went to White Agent and took the money.

The Kansas Land was not the promised land.

Great Bear, my father, had said, ". . . a land where White Ones would not threaten."

In the spring, it was time for the payments of the money. My father went again to White Agent. He returned, his face angry.

"White Ones change their words. They make a

wooden building and call it school. They say our children must go there to learn the White Ones' ways. Until we do this, they will not pay what they promised."

"We will have need of White Ones' money. There was no harvest of the corn," my mother spoke.

"They have the land. We will not give our children."

"What do the others do? The Ottawa? The Kansas? Chippewa?"

"The others are not Mesquakie."

"The others will live," my mother said. "The Mesquakie will starve."

I raised my voice in the family council. "Good father. I could go to the school. I am your child. Perhaps one Mesquakie will be enough."

So I joined the others, the Ottawa, the Kansas, the Chippewa, and went to the White Ones' school—one day. It *was* enough.

We sat on benches made of wood, hard and polished like stones washed often by the rain. We were in rows like planted corn and not in circles. We were not to move.

Gray Gull taught but one. White Teacher taught many.

White Teacher was strange. His eyes were pale, like the sky when clouds hide the color. His hair was yellow like wild mustard. His lips were thin and opened like the carp when it lies upon the river bank, snared by a spear.

He held up the White Ones' flag and said, "A-mer-i-ca. A-mer-i-ca."

We repeated, "A-mer-i-ca. A-mer-i-ca."

Then he pointed at each of us and said, "A-mer-i-can," and each one said it after him.

He pointed to me. "A-mer-i-can. A-mer-i-can."

"Mes-quak-ie," I said.

We did this many times until he became very red and then he decided to name stones.

He placed the stones in a row on the platform, and as he set them down he called them, "One. Two. Three. Four. Five."

He did it again and again and the others repeated his words. He pointed to each and each said the words. He pointed to me. I did not speak. Why would I name stones? I could grow old and blind naming just the stones in Stony Creek.

I sat on a high stool in a corner the rest of the day. Everyone could see that I was Mesquakie.

I learned other words that day: *uncivilized, papoose, squaw.* They were not pretty words.

I spoke to my father, Great Bear. "I can go no more to White Ones' school. Though we must starve, I cannot go. Un-civ-il-ized."

"What is that strange word you speak?"

"It is not good. I learned of it today in White Ones' school."

We learned many White Ones' words upon the reservation. I understood them, but spoke them little. I think my father, too, learned White Ones' words, but like the possum playing dead, he pretended not to know.

My father went again to White Agent to take the payment.

Again he returned, his face angry.

"White Ones change their words again. Our children will not go to White Ones' school. Then our children must go to White Ones' church. Until we do this, they will not pay what they promised."

"I will go with Hidden Doe to church," my mother said. "We have need of food."

We sat on benches made of wood. We were in rows like planted corn.

The Church Teacher was strange. Brown hair like tail of squirrel covered his mouth. His eating would be dirty for he had not plucked his hair. No Mesquakie man lets hair stay on his face.

He pointed to a drawing on the wall. A sad man hung from logs, and nails were in his hands and feet and thistles on his head. It was cruel. A Mesquakie would not do that, even to a Sioux.

He chanted long. Three words I learned: "God. Jesus. Holy Ghost."

Then they gave us food. The food was strange. The White Ones ate with tiny spears such as we would use for fish in Stony Creek. We waited for the dancing. There was no dancing. There was no drum, no rattles. The church was not a happy place.

I spoke to my father. "I can go no more to White Ones' church. Though we may starve, I cannot go. They speak of many gods. Un-civ-il-ized."

For the third time, my father went to White Agent to take the payment.

Again he returned, his face angry.

"White Ones change their words another time. Our children will not go to White Ones' school. Our people will not go to White Ones' church. Now they say we must appear before White Agent and name ourselves to him for winter count. This is not good! Until we do this, they will not pay what they promised."

"But, father," I spoke. "We are one. We are Mesquakie."

"White Ones do not understand. They name us wrong. They name us Fox. They name us Indian. We are Mesquakie. They can not learn." He rose and left our lodge, muttering, "Un-civ-il-ized."

My father did not go the fourth time to White Agent to receive our payment. White Agent came to us. He was a new White Agent. We did not see the other one again.

The Kansas Land was not the promised land.

Great Bear, my father, had said, "a land with flowing rivers and wooded hills and rich earth ready for the planting, of Bluecoats waiting to feed us and give us seed for the planting in the new land, of deer and antelope and buffalo, of land where neither Sioux nor White would threaten."

It was not so.

EIGHT

WE WERE PICKING the first ripe corn, my mother, Soft Cloud, and I.

"The corn ripens as you, my daughter, ripen. You have seen seventeen summers. Soon you may desire to take a husband. Whoever that will be, he alone is the one with whom you talk, when you begin to talk to men."

I hid my face among the corn leaves and picked the ears more quickly, for I thought at once of Black Crow. Laughing Wind had told me he was gone.

"I have not seen the one with whom I wish to talk," I assured my mother.

"That is good," my mother said. "Our young men are no longer as they were upon our Iowa. We women stay the same. We do as we have always done: we build our homes, we tend our fields, we cook our food, we bear our children. But what is there for our men? We have no need for hunters on this reservation. We have no need for warriors on this reservation."

Later my mother and I sat before our lodge and

60

shelled the new corn kernels from the cob with the old clam shells we had carried from Iowa.

"Be careful," my mother said. "Remember each grain of corn has feelings like you and I. If we waste them when we take them from the cob, they feel sad and weep. Corn is the food of our people. Mesquakies can travel far and work hard on little but corn."

My mother raised her head. "See. There goes the drunken one again. Look how he weaves upon his pony. He cannot ride. He does not see."

I looked where she pointed. It was Black Crow. His pony hung its head. The day was hot, and lather spun down from its lips.

Black Crow slid from his pony and stumbled into the lodge of one who often raced with the young braves.

"That is one with whom you should *not* talk," my mother said.

I did not answer.

The shelling of the corn was done. I stood to lay the cobs for drying. We would use them for our fire.

One ran shouting from the lodge where Black Crow was. White Agent came. His face showed fear. The medicine man of the White Ones came. They stayed long. My mother joined the women who gathered by the lodge. I made the fire and cooked our evening meal, and yet she lingered.

When she returned, she said, "It is the pox. The White Ones' pox. Black Crow dies."

My mother, my father, my uncle, and my aunt ate. I did not. I brought the water. I gathered wood. I cleaned the bowls. The time for sleeping came. Only then, lying alone upon my blanket, did I think of Black

Crow. He was not a hunter. He was not a warrior. And so he did not die a Yellow Earth Man.

White Agent came and talked long with my father.

My father told us, "Young Black Crow brings death to us. In white villages where he lodged he got the poison. It is the pox. White Ones call it *Small Pox*. It is sickness for White Ones. It is death for us."

"What does White Agent say?" Soft Cloud asked.

"White Agent says white medicine man would give each one of us a little of the sickness and we do not die."

"This can not be!" my mother cried. "He would poison all, because one was poisoned. I cannot understand."

"Those are the ways of White Ones. They are not ours," my father, Great Bear, said and spoke no more to us nor to White Agent.

Soon one came to my mother and said, "Bright Feather, friend of Gray Gull, sickens with the pox. Come."

For many sleeps our lodge was empty without my mother. While she was gone, my quiet brother sickened and lay upon his blanket talking of strange dreams and tearing at his chest.

My mother came back to our lodge. "Bright Feather is no more," she said, and turned to tend my brother.

Yellow Earth Women gathered around my mother when she came out from the poisoned lodge. "See," they said. "We do not sicken. We took the 'little sickness' from the White Ones. See upon our arms the mark."

My mother turned her back upon them.

The pox appeared upon my brother's face and his

eyes clouded with fever. I kept the fire and brewed the herbs as Gray Gull had taught me while our medicine man shook the sacred rattles and chanted long to bring the healing.

"Go not back into our lodge, Hidden Doe," my mother said. "It is full of White Ones' poison. Build yourself a lodge away. Sleep there with your aunt and uncle. There you will fast as long as your brother holds the poison."

White Agent came, holding a cloth across his mouth, and summoned my father.

"Great Bear," he said, his voice muffled. "I send our doctor to you. You must receive the medicine. You must open your lodge. Pull back the bearskin from the door."

"You would give us more poison? One from the pox and another from the spirit that roams at night and pours evil into the mouths of sleepers. The spirit will not enter if the bearskin hangs upon our door. We will not pull the bearskin aside. If we must die, we die the Mesquakie way."

"But the pox does not ask for names. It comes to all. Yet, see we who take the 'little sickness,' as you call it, live. Mesquakies die."

"As long as one Mesquakie lives, so do we all. We will not take the White Ones' medicine." My father turned his back on White Agent and walked away.

The sickness left my brother. The sickness entered my mother.

Each day I went to the door of our lodge and talked with the woman who cared for her.

"Leave me, Hidden Doe. Do not come to me," I heard my mother call from the darkened lodge.

After seven suns, she called no more.

My aunt came to me and said, "Soft Cloud has gone. Keep a silent heart."

That day I lost sight of the sun.

We fasted for my mother. On the fourth day, Great Bear, my father, sickened and went into our lodge.

It was then he said, "We have not strayed from the Mesquakie way even though I too am now taken by the poison. You, my daughter, are untouched. Nor does the pox touch your aunt and uncle. I thought long, sitting before our lodge as your mother's spirit loosed itself. Your brother still lies weak. I am taken with the sickness. This you must do. You who are well must leave this place. You, your aunt, your uncle, and a young brave proven on the hunt. Go back to the Iowa. You are my seed. The seed must be saved for the planting."

My uncle spoke, "But already the snows come from the north."

"Our ponies are strong. You and young Eye-of-Wolf will hunt. The women will follow. The rivers are frozen for crossing."

"But what of White Ones who live on the land?"

"Do not travel with the sun. Hide as Gray Gull does on the Iowa. Move when blackness comes. You will know the way. Where Mesquakie feet have stepped, that way is theirs."

And so it was.

In the darkness of our leaving, I crept to my father's lodge and pushed back the bearskin.

"My father," I whispered.

"Do not come into the lodge." He spoke hoarsely.

"We leave. Do you have words for Gray Gull, my grandmother?"

"You are my words. You are a Red Earth Woman. Go and find a way to bring our people home. This is no promised land for the Mesquakie."

We spoke no more.

Grandmother Moon showed us the way to the river. We moved silently among the leafless trees. I looked back but once. I could not see the lodges of our village, only our dark trail through the snow.

For six sleeps we met no one. We ate of the dried corn and small game that my uncle and Eye-of-Wolf hunted. We camped the seventh sun. My aunt and I rested while the men hunted. They returned at dusk with a young deer. Two more suns we stayed and prepared the meat and scraped the hide, which I carried on my back.

The sky became without sun and we grew more bold. Still we saw no one. The river lay behind us and the land, snow-covered, blinded us. At times we wandered long in search of trees for shelter. We are people of the woods, and the flat Kansas Land was not our grandmother.

The venison was gone before we reached the river of the Missouri.

"We hunt today," my uncle said. "We have seen no game for many suns. The hunt will be long."

My aunt nodded. "It is good. We have the river. We will build a lodge and wait."

My aunt and I built our lodge strong and tight. "Snow comes," my aunt said. "I have seen it in the sky."

And it was so.

My aunt and I waited beside the River of the Missouri as the snows blew hard against our lodge. There was no sun for many days. The land and sky were one. And still we waited. We huddled in our blankets and spoke little of our fear.

The sun returned.

"Now they come. The sun will guide them to us," I said.

"We will not speak of them. We wait."

We waited long and ate little. Cold Moon thaws came and then the snows returned.

"We wait no longer," said my aunt. "We move on. The men will find our way."

Together we crossed the frozen Missouri, climbed the bluffs and stood once more upon our Iowa Land. It was as if I were a child and Gray Gull held me.

My uncle and Eye-of-Wolf did not return. We moved on, safe among the rolling hills. I snared a rabbit with a noose made from the deerskin I carried. We camped against a creek bank to hide our fire from the White Ones' lodge which we had passed. And I prepared a stew.

"I grow weary," said my aunt and motioned the bowl away.

"We will stay another sun, my aunt," I said. "It will be easier for my uncle and Eye-of-Wolf to find us."

"Speak not of them. They will not come."

I lay beside my aunt that night and thought of Gray Gull. When I arose in the morning, my aunt lay still. Her face was marked with pox.

"You sicken. Tell me what to do. I have no herbs."

"Go from me quickly," she whispered. "Seek the White Ones whose lodge we passed. They will not harm you. Tell them not of me nor of the pox. Tell them you are alone and lost and ask of them the way back to Kansas Land."

"I cannot go. I cannot leave you."

"Your father, Great Bear, spoke to us and said, 'You are the seed.' You must be saved for the planting. I am but the husk. Now go."

I stayed with her until the sun moved down the sky. Then I built the fire high. I set the bowl beside her. I put my blanket over her. I left to find the White Ones' lodge.

NINE

SHE WAS STANDING in the snow chopping wood with a heavy axe that glistened in the sun. When she saw me, she stopped, buried the axe in the log, and waited for me, shading her eyes with mittened hand.

I stopped at the fence and leaned against the post, for I had hurried and the snow was deep.

"Lost." I spoke the White Ones' word.

The woman stepped back and rested one hand on the handle of the axe. "You alone? Where are the others?"

"Alone. Lost," I repeated.

"Who are your people? Where are they?"

"Mesquakie."

"You mean Fox?"

"Mesquakie," I said.

"Same thing. Land sakes, girl. You're supposed to be down on a reservation in Kansas. What you doing clear up here?"

"Alone," I repeated.

"You haven't got a blanket or nothing. Where you been sleeping? You can't be alone."

"Alone," I said again and pointed back toward the creek.

She watched me and then shook her head.

"Bet you're hungry and cold. Come on in the house. I'll fix you a cup of tea and some bread. Just baked a batch this morning." She wiped her face with the mittened hand. "Come on. Don't hang there by the fence. A body can freeze standing out here." She walked over to me, opened the wooden gate, and motioned toward the lodge.

It was the same as the White Ones' lodge beside Stony Creek except it was warm and full of color—on the sleeping platform, on the walls, even on the floor.

"Go on, sit down."

I squatted before the fire.

She was taller than my father and her hair was white as new snow. Her eyes were black like mine, and her mouth smiled even when she worked.

"Can't believe you. Walking around in this weather alone. Without a blanket yet. Never saw an Indian without a blanket. What's your name? Your name, I said. Your name?"

"Mesquakie."

"I know that. I mean you. You. Your name?" and she jabbed her finger under my nose.

I pointed at her and said, "A-mer-i-can."

The woman threw back her head and laughed, and all of her shook. "Yes, American. My name is Gwen. Gwen Evans, but I suppose that's too much of a mouthful for you. G---wen," and she pointed to herself.

"G---wen," I repeated, and she laughed again.

"Your name. And don't tell me Mesquakie again. Name?" and she pointed at me.

"Hidden Doe," I said.

"Hidden Doe? Well. That's quite a name. I'll call you Doe. That all right? Tea's ready now. Could you sit up at the table? The table," and she patted the stool.

I remembered how my mother and I had eaten at the church place in Kansas Land. I got up. A cloth of flowers as real as spring covered the table. There was a spoon and a bowl, but no spear. There was white bread with golden top. I did not hesitate. I ate the bread, tearing it into pieces and stuffing it into my mouth.

"Sakes alive, child! You must be starved. When's the last time you ate? Take your time. There's more. But don't eat yourself sick."

"No! No!" I stopped chewing. "Not sick! Alone. Not sick!"

I gulped the hot tea.

"Good?" she asked.

"Good," I answered.

"Tea's best medicine I know."

I set the bowl down. "Not sick. No." I could drink no more.

"You say you're Mesquakie? Been hearing about you Indians down there on that reservation. Having a bad time what with the pox and all."

"No! No pox!" I held out my arms and shook my head.

"Drink up. Your tea's getting cold. Pox don't scare me. Look," and she pulled back her sleeve. Her arm was big and very white. The mark of the "little sickness" was on it.

She stood up, wrapped herself in a heavy coat, and tied a cloth about her head. "We'll get to the bottom of this. Come. We'll follow your tracks. Here. Put this blanket around you. Come."

I followed her from the lodge and through the snow where I had walked.

"Oh, child," she cried as she knelt and pulled the blankets aside and looked at my aunt's face.

With one swoop, the White One gathered my aunt in her arms and started back toward the log lodge. "No living thing must be left to die in the snow. I wouldn't do that to an Englishman. Come bring your traps and let's get this woman into the house."

I spread my blanket before the fire, and the White Woman laid my aunt gently upon it.

"She's pretty well gone. Get her some tea." She pointed to my bowl.

I held the bowl to my aunt's lips, while the White Woman, her big hands weathered as dark as my own, sponged my aunt's forehead with a cloth, muttering, "There, dearie. That feel better? Drink a little of that tea. Drink up. Now, that wasn't so bad, was it?"

My aunt's eyes opened and widened at the white face above her, then closed. She slept.

"You sleep, too, child. I'll watch. She your mother? Mother? Mother?" and she pointed to me.

I shook my head. "Mesquakie."

"Have it your way then. Mesquakie. But at least she must be your kin. Your men? Where are they? Braves? Warriors? Hunters?"

"Lost," I said. "Snow."

"Oh, now you're beginning to make some sense." The White Woman talked always loud. "You left the reservation with the pox. Men got lost. Where were you going? Where were you headed? No Indians around here anymore that I know of. Where? Where?"

"Iowa," I said and pointed where the sun would rise.

"You're in Iowa, child. This is Iowa. We been a state since '46."

"River."

"River? You mean the Iowa River? Clear over there. Why, you're one of the bunch that went through here to Kansas three or four years ago with the soldiers. You sneaking back?"

She talked more but I was very tired and I did not understand all her words.

"Land, child. Listen to me going on. You must be bushed. Curl up there by the fire. Here. Use this clean blanket. I'll see to your mother, or whoever she is. Now sleep."

I awoke once in the night. The White Woman was bending over my aunt. My aunt's clothes hung drying before the fire, and the woman was washing the naked body.

When I awoke again in the morning, my aunt was gone. The White Woman sat in a chair across from me. When she saw that I was awake, she spoke. "She is dead, poor soul. Dead. Can you understand?"

I nodded. I knew the word well.

"There's just us here to do the burying, Doe. My man won't be back from the trading post for another week or so. We can't wait that long even in this weather. Eat. Then come. I got her outside the door. She's all right."

As we went out into the cold, she pointed. "Bring that axe there and that shovel."

I followed her as she carried my aunt, wrapped in our blanket, down a small slope behind the log lodge.

"Here." She lay my aunt in the snow. "This south slope won't be froze as hard." She shoveled the snow away.

I looked around. There were three piles of stones and three wooden crosses. It was the White Woman's burying ground.

Together we chopped the shallow grave and together we carried the stones.

When we were finished, she straightened up and brushed the snow from her skirt. "Don't suppose you're Christian. Must have some religion of your own. Doesn't matter. We're all heading the same place. But if you don't mind, I'll do it my way. Only way I know."

She began to sing, in a sad, sad chant with words that were not of the White Ones. It sounded almost like the words of our Red Earth People.

Mwy a mwy
Mwy a mwy
Mwy a mwy
Yn canlyn

When she had finished, she looked down at me and smiled. "Bet you've never heard singing like that before. Sounds like an old goose hissing, doesn't it? Well, it's Welsh. Welsh, girl. That's what I am." She picked up the axe and the shovel. "You say you're not Fox. You're

Mesquakie. Well, I'm not American. I'm Welsh. And I think you and me are going to get along just fine."

Together we walked back to the White Woman's lodge.

"Now," she said, as she pulled off her heavy coat. "Let's get you cleaned up. Why you haven't got the pox, I'll never know." She pulled back my sleeve and looked at my arms. "Didn't they vaccinate you Indians down there? Thought I heard they did."

"Mesquakie," I said and pulled down my sleeve.

"Well, Mesquakie or not, you're going to have a bath." She took a heavy wooden pail and filled it with hot water from the pot over the fire.

"Now," she said, holding out a soft yellow stone, "here's the soap. Here's a washrag. And here's a towel. Now get those clothes off and scrub. It might not keep you from getting the pox, but it couldn't hurt."

I smelled the soft yellow stone. I looked into the wooden pail. There was too much water to drink. I looked up at her and shook my head.

"I'm not getting through to you, am I? Well, I suppose I need a bath as much as you. Do what I do."

She took off her heavy moccasins and then pointed to mine. She wore cloths over her feet. I handed her my moccasins. I thought she desired them as a gift.

She laughed and pulled off her skirt, and another skirt, and another skirt, and many more cloths until she was wearing nothing. Her whiteness frightened me.

"Come on, girl. Now here's the way you do it. See." She dipped the yellow stone in the water and rubbed it on her body. Then I knew it was the cleansing. I had no need for the cleansing. The stream was for my cleansing.

"Take them off. Take them off. Do as I do."

I turned my back to her. I could not watch. It was not the Mesquakie way. I curled up by the fire.

Then I felt the big hands of the White Woman in my hair. She lifted me as if I were a child, stripping my clothes away, and plunged me feet first into the wooden pail.

She held me with one hand and scrubbed me with the other, even my hair. Then she pushed me toward the fire and handed me a cloth to dry myself.

"There now, that's better. Sit there by the fire. I don't want you to get a chill. I'm going to get rid of these clothes of yours. Ought to burn them. Probably full of pox."

She gave me a shirt such as Black Crow had worn. "Here. This'll do for awhile. Keep you warm at least. My man's not much bigger than you. And this old skirt of mine should work if I hitch it up here. Now, let me comb out that hair of yours."

"No. No," I screamed and ran from her.

"What's wrong, child? I won't hurt you. Just want to comb out that hair," and she made motions of combing her own.

"No," I cried, my back against the door.

"Well, this time, *I* don't understand."

I walked over to her, took the strange comb from her hand, and, in the Mesquakie way, went outside to comb my hair. She watched me from the doorway, nodding and smiling. "We have much to learn from each other, my Doe."

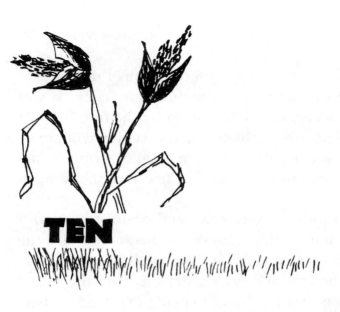

TEN

I STAYED with Gwen, the White Woman, for there was no place for me to go. The snows came again, but it was warm in the lodge. I learned her words, for she spoke always as summer leaves do in wind.

"That Doe name of yours. Do you mind if I call you *Dorothy?* Had a Dorothy once. 'Bout your age. She lies there with your kin on the south slope. Do you mind the name? Dorothy?"

"Dorothy," I repeated and smiled.

She was much for smiling. When she was not smiling, she was talking, and when she was not talking, she was singing. Her lodge was a warm place.

"G---wen," I said and shook my head. "Do not like. Cannot speak. G---wen. White Gull?"

"White Gull! You know about gulls? Why, when I was a girl in Wales, I used to sit for hours and watch the gulls come in from the sea. White Gull? I like that," and she patted me on the arm. "Yes. I will be White Gull and you will be Dorothy."

Sometimes, when she was not talking, she sat before the fire. "Snow's delayed my man. Guess I'll read awhile to keep my mind off him. Good man, my Johnluv."

"Johnluv," I repeated, not understanding.

"John to you, girl. Only I call him Johnluv. John."

"John," I said. "Man."

"Yes indeed, a man. Not a lot of him, but quality all the way. Here, girl. Sit here on the rug. I'll read you some of this. You probably won't understand it. Not sure I do myself, but the words sound nice. Here's one my Johnluv likes."

And she read:

Shall I compare thee to a summer's day?
Thou art more lovely and more temperate:
Rough winds do shake the darling buds of May,
And summer's lease hath all too short a date:

The words were like the summer sounds along our River Iowa.

She read on:

Sometimes too hot the eye of summer shines,
And often is his gold complexion dimm'd;

She broke off. "Listen! D'ya hear that?"

She bounded from her chair and grabbed the gun that hung over the fireplace. "Those pesky wolves are at my smokehouse again. I'll fix them."

She was out the door. I watched her rest the gun on the top rail of the fence and fire. She returned dragging a dead wolf by the tail. "Got him! On the first shot too.

Hate to waste a bullet on the varmints, but they're not going to eat my good meat."

It was a strange lodge where the woman was the hunter.

We turned to go back inside. It was then I saw a man riding over the snow-covered hill. He led a pack horse.

"Bluecoat! I hide by the creek."

She caught my arm. "Soldiers have better things to do these days than hunt down one Mesquakie girl. That's no Bluecoat. That's my Johnluv back from trading."

He was a small man, not big enough for either a hunter or warrior. Gray curly hair covered his head. He had eyes that flashed like a raccoon's at night.

He jumped down from his horse, a big horse, and put his arms around White Gull. His head fit under her chin.

"Snow held me up, Gwenny, or I'd been here a week ago. How ya been?" He turned and looked at me. "Who's this? Where'd you find her?"

"This is Dorothy. She found me."

"Mesquakie," I said, as he grabbed my hand and shook it up and down.

It was a strange greeting.

"Well, let's not stand out here in the cold. The two of you hike inside while I carry this stuff in and tend to the horses."

And he did. When he was through with that, he brought the water and the firewood.

It was a strange lodge where the man did woman's work.

I slept before the fire in the White Woman's lodge on a new blanket that she sewed for me. I had tried to sleep upon the White Ones' platform as she told me, but I could not, for I felt smothered in its softness.

That night, when White Gull's Raccoon-Man returned, I lay before the fire and listened to their voices. I could not sleep. Sadness chewed at my heart.

I thought of Laughing Wind and the marks from the White Ones' fire on our wrists. I remembered summer nights along the Iowa and of my family talking in quiet voices around the fire. I thought of Soft Cloud, my mother, gone, and of my quiet aunt lying with the strange White Ones and no one to guide her spirit, of my father, Great Bear, and the sickness. Had his spirit fled too?

With Raccoon-Man home, there was little for me to do. He brought the water, he carried the wood, he built the fire, he even cooked the tea and brought it to White Gull and me. Most strange of all, he showed us the seeds he had brought from the trader and told us of *his* plans for the planting in the spring.

"You plant seeds?" I asked Raccoon-Man.

"You bet your boots, I do. Plant 'em. Weed 'em. Harvest 'em."

"And he's a dandy farmer, too," White Gull added.

I shook my head and said, "Un-civ-i-lized."

White Gull and Raccoon-Man laughed loudly and told the story to each other over and over.

It was a strange lodge where story-telling was for laughter. Mesquakie stories are for teaching.

My hands became idle in the White Woman's lodge. Then I remembered Gray Gull's words when she

instructed me in the twenty suns of becoming a woman:
Share with others the things you make.

I had slept by the White Ones' fire. My aunt rested
in the White Ones' burying ground. I had grown fat on
White Ones' food. Mesquakies share. I had only taken. I
would make the deerskin into moccasins for Raccoon-
Man, for he often walked within the lodge in bare feet.

Planting time neared, and the light of day grew
longer as I worked. I had no beads. When White Gull
saw what I was doing, she said, "Here. Use some of
John's seed corn for decoration. He'll never miss it."

It was a strange lodge where seeds were wasted on
moccasins.

Then came the time for me to go again to my little
wickiup, as it comes in each moon to all who have become women. I rose early, before White Gull or Raccoon-Man stirred. I took corn and dried meat and my
old garments which the White Woman had not burned,
but instead had boiled and scrubbed and hung in the
winter sun.

I hurried to the creek. There I built my wickiup
against the bank, yet far from the one where the sickness
had been. All day I fasted. Many times I heard White
Gull call, "Dorothy! Dorothy! Where are you?"

And Raccoon-Man, too: "Dorothy! Dorothy!" I
dared not answer.

The sun was almost hidden when I heard White
Gull's steps.

"My child! What on earth are you doing out here?
It's below zero. What have we done? Come home! You'll
freeze. John! Here she is."

I called from the small wickiup. "He must not come. It is not good."

"Is it the pox, child?" White Gull shouted. "You will not harm us."

"Not pox. It is that time with me when the Mesquakie woman must be alone."

I heard Raccoon-Man approach.

"Go back to the house, John. This is between us women. I'll be up later."

He left.

White Gull stooped low and crawled into my wickiup. There was hardly room for two of us.

"Nothing to be ashamed of, girl. Happens to all of us. This the first time? Are you afraid?"

"No, White Gull. I have lived seventeen summers."

"Then what are you doing out here? Why do you run from us?"

We sat long in the little wickiup and I told her of our ways. Then White Gull told me of hers.

The dark had been with us for many hours before White Gull crept from my small wickiup. "I'd never make it doing it your way, girl. Got a crick in my back already. But you stay here. Do it your way. Who's to say what's right? Don't know but what it wouldn't be a good idea for every woman to get off by herself for a few days every month. Anyway, you come back to us when you're ready."

And White Gull left me.

ELEVEN

THE TIME of planting neared. I could no longer eat the White Ones' food. I could no longer drink the tea.

"Something wrong, girl?" Raccoon-Man asked. "You sick?"

White Gull touched my forehead. "It's not a sickness of the body. It's something else. Homesick, maybe. Is that it, Dorothy?"

I nodded. "I long for my people."

"See, I told you, Johnluv." White Gull looked at Raccoon-Man. "She wants to go home. I know just how she feels. If it weren't for you, I'd have given up long time ago on this Iowa business and gone back to my own Welsh hills. Besides, John, she needs friends her own age."

"I know," Raccoon-Man said. "Spring's coming. It's a restless time."

"It's more than that, John. You know how corn won't grow down in that lower field. But you can get a good crop of oats off it? Same with people. They got to grow in their own place. In their own way." She turned

82

to me. "So you want to go back to the reservation, Dorothy?"

"No. I go to my grandmother on the Iowa."

"Grandmother?" White Gull bellowed. "How come she's not down in Kansas?"

"She hides from Bluecoats. She would not leave the Iowa."

"She's a Mesquakie, I can see," White Gull laughed and slapped her knee.

"Yes," I answered, smiling too, "Mesquakie."

"Your grandmother have a name? Or is she like your kin up there on the hill. You never did tell me who she was or what she was called. But maybe that's the Mesquakie way. And that's all right too."

I looked at her. "Gray Gull," I said.

"Gray Gull," the woman repeated softly. "What a beautiful name. Your grandmother, you say?"

"Yes. Gray Gull, my grandmother."

"And you named *me* White Gull?"

"White Gull," I repeated.

She turned and looked at Raccoon-Man. He smiled. Then as if she had suddenly remembered something, she went to her shelf by the fireplace and clattered among her tea cups, her back to me.

"Grandmother or not," Raccoon-Man said. "We're not letting you traipse out to the Iowa alone."

"I go to the Iowa."

White Gull turned to us. "No, Dorothy. You listen. Listen to John. He knows what he's talking about."

"You can't go by yourself, girl. First of all, the state's full of homesteaders. If they don't see you and send you back to Kansas, the soldiers will. Besides, it's too far for a girl to go alone, anyway. We wouldn't think of letting you start out."

"He's right, Dorothy. A woman your age isn't safe, travelling alone. Wolves aren't the only varmints we have on the frontier. Now, the only sensible thing for you to do is to go back and see your people in Kansas."

"My father sent me to my grandmother."

"I know, Dorothy, but as near as I can understand, he sent you with three other people. He didn't send you alone."

I nodded. It was so.

"Now why can't you," she continued, "go back to Kansas the same way you came and have some of your people bring you back to Iowa?"

"Either way, Gwen, it's a long way for Dorothy here to walk." He looked at me. "I'd like to have you stay with us, Dorothy. The house'll be empty without you."

I did not know that men spoke aloud such feelings. It puzzled me.

"I think, John, Dorothy's set on going. I've always said the biggest part of loving is letting go. Now, we've got that extra horse there in the barn that's eating us out of house and home. You don't need him for planting. Why not give him to Dorothy when she goes back to visit her people?"

"I need no horse. It is our braves and chiefs who need horses."

"Well, you said your father is a chief, didn't you?" White Gull argued.

"I know not if he lives."

"Got any brothers?" Raccoon-Man asked.

"I have but one."

"Well, that's it. Easy as pie. We'll send your brother the horse. And you're doing us a favor by taking it. . . . You do know the way back?"

"Where Mesquakie feet have stepped, that way is theirs," I answered.

"Even so, John, though she *does* know, she can't go all the way by herself. Take her to the ferry. See she gets across. Then she'll turn south till she hits the Osage. Not too many white settlements there; she shouldn't have any trouble."

So it was decided.

When the time of leaving came, my mouth was dry as if with thirst and I could speak no words.

I followed Raccoon-Man. I rode away and left my quiet aunt upon the slope among the White Ones' graves. I rode away and left White Gull standing alone in the doorway of her lodge. I could not look back at her.

We had been long together.

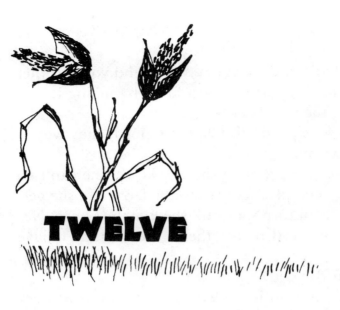

TWELVE

THE WOMEN were in our field preparing for the planting when I returned to the Kansas Land. I tethered Raccoon-Man's horse behind our lodge.

I spoke to a child playing in the sand with her corn husk doll, "Where is the son of Great Bear?"

She pointed to the far end of the village. "He is there with Great Bear and the others."

"My father lives?" I asked, but the child did not reply.

I took the hoe from the lodge and joined our women in the field.

"Hidden Doe!" called Laughing Wind. The women left their hoeing and gathered around me while I told them of my uncle, of Eye-of-Wolf, and of my aunt.

"Your father, Great Bear, speaks now with one sent from your grandmother, Gray Gull," Laughing Wind said. "She sends her words. Tonight we hear."

I hoed in the fields until the sun was low. I gathered the wood for my father's fire and carried it back to our lodge. The woman who had been with my mother said, "I cared for your mother, Soft Cloud, when she sickened. I cared for your father, Great Bear, when you were gone. You have come back. I return now to my own lodge."

My father came and sat within our lodge. I brought the food which I had prepared and set it before him.

His face was scarred from the pox. His eyes sad. He took the food from me and said, "So the seed is saved. It is good. Word has come from Gray Gull. Sit in your mother's place with the women tonight and you will hear."

I told him of my journey, of my uncle and Eye-of-Wolf, of my aunt. And then I spoke of White Gull and Raccoon-Man and of the horse.

He sat silent until his food was gone. Then he said, "We will take the White Ones' horse." He said no more.

He did not speak aloud his feelings. It puzzled me.

My people gathered for the council.

The one sent by Gray Gull, my grandmother, was called Bright Eagle. He was slender as the birch sapling and graceful as the willow, yet when he spoke, his voice was deep like distant thunder.

"These are the words Gray Gull told me to speak," he began. " 'We are Mesquakie. We are the people who were created first. The earth is our grandmother. She calls. Come back. The spirits of the children who are buried call. Come back. White Ones would scatter us like seeds thrown to the wind. This must not be. We are one. We are Mesquakie.' " Bright Eagle paused. Great Bear nodded. The men and women of the council nodded. I watched the face of Bright Eagle.

" 'Long have we watched the White Ones,' " Bright

Eagle continued with Gray Gull's words. " 'Long have we sought a way. When we hunt the possum, we learn of its ways. Only then can we snare it. We eat of the possum. We do not become the possum. White Ones buy our Iowa Land. It cannot be taken from them. No Bluecoats drive them from it. Red Earth People can buy Iowa Land. It cannot be taken from us. No Bluecoats can drive us from it. This is the way. That is all.' And so Gray Gull instructed me to speak."

Bright Eagle finished his words. No one spoke.

Hunters could learn of possum ways. They did not become possums. I had learned of White Gull's ways. I was still Mesquakie. My grandmother's words were good.

Great Bear spoke. "They have taken from us. Now we will use their money to buy from them."

One spoke, "We have long bought from White Ones: guns, bullets, food, cloth, beads. Yet we have nothing. How will this be different?"

"It is land," spoke Bright Eagle. "A bullet fired is gone. Guns break and rust. Food is eaten. Land endures."

"But," spoke the first, "we will need much of White Ones' money."

"Our seed is planted in the field," my father said. "Bring to me the money you have left. Meanwhile, taste not White Ones' whiskey, wager not on racing of ponies, chew well on scanty food."

One who had not spoken before said, "We could sell to White Ones: moccasins, beadwork, squashes, pumpkins, even our ponies, if we must. And bring the White Ones' money to Great Bear."

"And soon," said another, "the time comes for payment from White Agent."

"How can we give of our payment to Great Bear? We need the money for food. We will starve upon this reservation!"

"For this reason, *leave* the reservation!" spoke Bright Eagle, and many nodded.

"If we stay here, take their money, and buy their food, we are but maggots on the dead growing fat and pale. We must go. We will grow thin and poor, but we will live. We are Mesquakie." So said Great Bear, my father. "We will speak of this again."

I walked alone to my father's lodge and thought of my mother's words: "Soon you may desire to take a husband. Whoever that will be, he alone is the one with whom you talk." I had seen that one.

Bright Eagle came often to our lodge and talked long with my father. He did not speak to me, but I think he knew I was there.

I wondered, as I worked in the field, if he had a wife. As I hoed, I found that others wondered too. Laughing Wind boasted she would talk with him. My heart grew sore.

I longed, as I set the food before my father and Bright Eagle, to ask him of my grandmother, but I was a Red Earth Woman. It was not our way.

I was preparing the fried bread. My hands were white with dough as I kneaded. I was singing softly to myself, and I did not hear him approach our lodge.

"I would speak with Great Bear," he called from the entry.

I did not look up from my work. I knew his voice well.

"My father is not here."

"When will he return?"

"Soon."

I knew my father had gone to the next village to speak with the men about the Iowa Land and would be long in returning.

"I will wait for him outside."

I wanted to ask him to come into my lodge, for I would have looked upon his face, but I did not want him to think wrong of me.

He sat on the ground, just outside our entryway. As I worked, I could see the side of his face.

When the bread was prepared, I searched for other work to do that would keep me near him. It was long before he spoke.

"Gray Gull has spoken often to me of Hidden Doe."

"Gray Gull is well?" I asked. I had heard the words Bright Eagle brought from my grandmother that she was well, yet I longed to talk with this man.

"Gray Gull is well," he muttered. Then he spoke louder. "She speaks words of praise for Hidden Doe and her skills."

"Gray Gull is a good teacher. Where does Gray Gull build her lodge?"

"Along the Iowa." He paused. "I have heard of Hidden Doe's powers with the herbs that heal. It is good."

"Does my grandmother grow old?"

I waited long for his answer. I feared he would leave.

"Does my grandmother live alone?"

"We have spoken long enough of grandmothers. I would speak of *you.*"

It was this I wanted most. I did not know it could be so easy.

My father stayed long in the village. Bright Eagle stayed long outside my lodge.

After that time, I longed to see Bright Eagle.

The harvest feasts were small. Our Red Earth People ate the corn, bought little of the White Agent, and brought the money saved to my father, Great Bear. The White Ones' money filled the deerskin bag beneath my father's sleeping platform. Each night he counted the money, then rose and ate but little of the meal I had prepared. I too grew thin.

The harvest dance began. I wore my headband of the butterfly. My father drummed the beat. Of all the braves who danced, Bright Eagle was the strongest and the quickest. I watched only him.

I danced with the women, my eyes straight ahead, my face serious. Ahead of me, Laughing Wind danced. I thought she moved too freely.

Bright Eagle danced within our circle, his steps bringing him often close to Laughing Wind and me. I could not tell which one of us he saw. I feared it was she.

The dances were many that night. We danced long. I walked alone to my father's lodge as Grandmother Moon left the sky. No footsteps followed mine.

Bright Eagle and my father's brother, Little Bear, appeared at my father's lodge the next morning. I prepared the food, and while they ate, I listened to their words.

"Here is the money," my father said, bringing out the deerskin bag.

"How much?" asked Bright Eagle.

"Seven hundred, thirty, and five of White Ones' dollars."

"Is it enough?" my uncle asked.

"We do not know," my father answered. "Buy from the White Ones as much as they will sell."

"It will buy but little, yet it will be seed for the new planting," Bright Eagle said, and the others nodded.

"You, Bright Eagle and Little Bear, my brother, must travel long and far down the Iowa River to the home of the White Father of the Iowa Land. They name it 'Iowa City.' " My father paused. "There you will say, 'White Ones buy land. Mesquakie buy land.' Empty the bag before him. Let him count the money."

"It will be as you say," Bright Eagle answered and took the bag of money from my father.

"From there, go and seek out Roaring Thunder, who stays with Gray Gull far up on the Iowa. They will lead you to the land which will be ours. For this we have waited. Return, then, to Kansas and lead us home."

"We go," said Bright Eagle. Little Bear left our lodge. My father, Great Bear, followed. Bright Eagle stayed.

"I go with the others to buy the land," he said with eyes that saw me. "I go with heavy feet. I shall return to you with swift steps."

I scrubbed the bowls not knowing what my hands did. "I will wait. Time will be long."

"Talk not to other men. It would sorrow me."

Only once before had I heard a man speak aloud his feelings. This time I understood.

We did not touch, but for a moment we stood close.

The moons passed slowly through the winter snows and spring plantings. I stayed much within the lodge. I spoke to no men, though some would speak to me.

Laughing Wind said once to me, "It is dull without Bright Eagle here. He is missed at the dances."

I did not answer.

"There are those who would like to be with you. My brother, Rushing Cloud, has said your name to my mother."

"I have no words for Rushing Cloud," I replied.

"You are sick for Bright Eagle," she teased. "Swim in the cold water of the Osage. That will cool your sickness. Then put on your headband and join us in the Snake Dance."

I did not wish to be cooled.

As my father and brother slept on their side of the lodge and I on mine, when sands held the heat of the Kansas sun through the night, I lay thinking of Bright Eagle and of my grandmother, Gray Gull, and of the promise of land along the Iowa.

I was long reaching sleep. A face came near to mine. I heard someone whisper, "Hidden Doe, I would talk with you."

I opened my eyes. Even in the darkness I knew it was Rushing Cloud, for I had often heard his bragging in the village.

"I have a pony. Swiftest of all ponies in the races. I am a fine hunter though the game be few. I fear no

Sioux nor Cheyenne nor Comanche. I would treat you well. Would you talk with me?"

I turned from him and did not speak. He said no more but waited for my voice. When it did not come, he left. No one but Rushing Cloud would know that I refused his courting. It is the way of our people. It is kind.

The hot days lingered. My eyes wearied from searching the flat land for Little Bear, my father's brother, and the others. I waited for news of Gray Gull, my grandmother. I longed for Bright Eagle.

In the Moon of the Elk, I lay alone on my blanket. I was long reaching sleep. Then I heard his voice outside our lodge. My father and brother rose and went to him. They talked in whispers. I crept to the entry so that I could look upon his face. They huddled on the ground around him, and I listened.

"The land is ours. I have the White Ones' paper." His voice was tired.

"The money was enough?" It was my father.

"No. We left the White Father of Iowa and went to Roaring Thunder and Gray Gull. She travelled far among our people, scattered along the Iowa, to get the money. Many sold their ponies to the White Ones and brought the dollars to her."

"It is good," my father said. "And what of the land?"

All were shadows bent toward each other, but Bright Eagle stood out from the rest.

"To the White Ones, the land is not much. Eighty-acres, they name it. It is seed from which a larger plant can grow. It is by the Iowa. There are hills. And trees.

White Ones do not fence it. There is no White Agent there. It is no reservation. It is our land."

"It is so," agreed the others.

"What of White Ones who will surround us?"

"They are not our friends. They are not our enemies. One spoke with Gray Gull and signed words on a paper to help us."

I smiled in the darkness of the lodge. Truly my grandmother had studied the ways of the possum.

"The morning star rises. We will talk more upon the new day," my father said, and his voice was no longer heavy with age. "Then we decide who will be the first to go and build lodges upon our land."

I slipped back to my blanket and lay thinking until dawn while my father and brother slept.

Though Bright Eagle had not looked upon me, I knew that we would talk.

I walked early to the fields with Laughing Wind.

"The Bright One is back," she said. "Already he has visited our lodge."

"You talked with him?" I asked, too quickly.

"He spoke of the long journey. I will soon follow him to the Iowa Land."

"Is it decided who will go?" I did not turn to her, but looked far down the path to the field.

"Our lodge has ponies. Surely we will be among those who go. Too bad your father is the chief and you must stay."

"I need not always lodge with my father. I can return to my grandmother."

We spoke no more to each other and hoed in silence.

Bright Eagle spoke of our return to Iowa in many lodges. I walked often in the village, but saw him not. I feared his eyes no longer saw me.

I had much work to do within our lodge. The corn had not been ground. The sewing was not done. My beadwork was unfinished. There were moccasins to make.

One day he came.

I was bent over the cooking-pot cleaning the black ash from its sides.

"I would speak with Hidden Doe," he called from the entry.

I did not look up. "I must finish my work."

"Will the work be long?"

"It is almost done," I replied.

"I will wait."

He sat down *inside* my lodge.

As I worked, I could feel his eyes upon me. I did not scrub the pot long.

"Tell me of my grandmother, Gray Gull," I began, sitting down across the lodge from him.

"Today I do not speak of your grandmother. Today I speak of you. I have longed for you. I speak with many people, but think only of you. I have met many. I have traded often. I bring this." He held out a string of silver and turquoise beads. They were most beautiful.

"Such a gift can say many things," I said.

"I have many things to say to one who does not talk with every man."

I could not speak, but to myself I said, "I would share my life with such a man as this."

My father spoke to me the next day. "Gray Gull has

sent word that you should come to her. So it shall be. You will go with your uncle and your brother and the others. I must stay in Kansas to receive our payments. We will buy more land and I will come to you."

"If you stay in Kansas, who will lead us to Iowa?"

"Little Bear, my brother, and Bright Eagle, whom Gray Gull has trusted."

THIRTEEN

AT THAT TIME in autumn when the day and night are equally long, upon the full moon, we left the Kansas Land and the White Ones' reservation. We went silently, in small groups, so no one would see. We would be gone for the winter count, and we did not want Bluecoats to search for us.

We met, eleven lodges of us, at the headwaters of the Osage and turned our backs upon the reservation. We travelled only at night until we crossed the Missouri. The way was long, but our steps were swift. The bearskin for the winter lodge in Iowa was light upon my back.

When we reached the Iowa Land, we rested for two days and feasted and danced our thanksgiving. The game our hunters brought to us was small, but its taste was sweet. Laughing Wind was with us, but she talked now to one called Black Wolf, for Bright Eagle spoke only to me.

We moved on, but the White Ones' fences made the way long and crooked. At dusk we stopped to camp within a grove of trees, and we women began to gather wood for our fires. Three men, White Ones on horses with guns pointed skyward, rode into our camp.

Bright Eagle, who spoke the White Ones' words well, talked with them. He did not speak loudly. He did not speak long.

He came to us and said, "We cannot camp here. It is the White Ones' land as the land along the Iowa is ours. We move."

Quietly I said to him, "There is another place where we can stay. It is not far. I have been this way before."

"Lead us to this place," he said.

I followed the creek. We passed White Gull's lodge and Raccoon-Man's fields. We passed the little wickiup where White Gull had come to me. We passed the spot where my aunt and I had stayed. Then we camped.

"There is no need to hide our fires. The White Ones will not come," I said to Bright Eagle.

After we had eaten, Bright Eagle spoke to me alone. "You have been this way before?"

"I have lived with the White Ones of this land," and I told him of White Gull and Raccoon-Man. I told him of my aunt. And I told him of the horse my brother rode.

"The White Ones? Would you speak with them?" Bright Eagle asked.

"We were long together, White Gull and I. We learned much from each other. I carry her in my heart. We will not meet again."

"It is good," he said. "You are a wise one."

But when all slept, I rose from my blanket. I took the sacred tobacco from my pouch and walked again up from the creek, through Raccoon-Man's fields to the slope where my aunt lay.

The stones were as if newly placed. No grass nor thistle grew upon her grave. And where White Gull and I had laid my aunt, there stood a cross of wood with marks of White Ones' words upon it. In the way of our people, I sprinkled tobacco over my aunt's grave and saved a portion for each of White Gull's others.

I walked silent as the hunter, through the darkness up to White Gull's lodge. Nothing stirred. I was no stranger to this place.

I had thought long, since leaving the Missouri, of White Gull and Raccoon-Man. They had given much. I had given little. Now I had even less to give. White Gull had often spoken of my headband with the butterfly.

"My land, Dorothy. You made that. Why, you're an artist. I couldn't do that in a million years," and she had laughed at herself.

I would have given it to her when I left, but I could not bear to look into her eyes.

I had brought the headband with me, and now I hung it on the gate where first I spoke with White Gull.

We moved at dawn.

Bright Eagle spoke to me as he looked back. "That is the White Ones' lodge where you have stayed?"

I nodded, but I did not look to see. Instead I looked ahead and followed after my people.

The cold came early and the game fled before our hunters. We moved now in old trails of our winter hunts, past places we had camped. Before, we had the venison, the corn, and the dried roots, and our cooking pots were full. Now, with each step, our hunger grew.

Laughing Wind no longer talked with Black Wolf. Now she talked with my brother, for only he rode upon the White Ones' horse.

"Your brother would be a good husband," she said to me. "His horse is bigger and stronger than the ponies of the others. And when there was game, he hunted well."

I nodded. For many days I had watched as Laughing Wind walked beside my brother. On the roads of the White Ones when we met the strange wagons, Bright Eagle led the way; the rest of us walked behind in a long line, with my brother and Laughing Wind the last. Laughing Wind talked and laughed; my brother sometimes nodded.

"We move like a snake going backwards in the grass. If your brother led the way we would not be starving. Bright Eagle is an old man. He knows not new ways."

"What new ways?" I asked.

"Cannot you see? For three suns now, we have had no corn. Yet we pass the White Ones' fields heavy with ears. We could ask for corn from the White Ones. They would give it to us as the White Ones gave the horse."

"The horse was a gift. Mesquakies do not beg," I said, my voice rising.

"Those are words of an old woman. You and Bright Eagle are well matched." She slowed her steps and dropped behind me in the line.

That night, Laughing Wind parched corn in her fire.

Bright Eagle saw and said, "How is it that you have the White Ones' corn?"

"White Ones waste. They leave much in their fields.

It is left for animals," Laughing Wind said as she smiled and chewed the corn.

Bright Eagle frowned. "We do not beg of White Ones. We do not take from White Ones' fields."

"Then we starve before we get to our land. You speak always in the old way. We were each to have our own field on the reservation, yet Hidden Doe said that was not right, that the fields belong to all. I would have had a field of my own. Then I would have had corn to bring. Must it be the same on our Iowa Land?"

"Can you not see?" Bright Eagle spoke loudly. "It was the White Ones' way to divide us. Mesquakies are one. As one we will plant the Iowa Land."

"It is the old way. We will starve."

Bright Eagle nodded. "Yes, it is the old way. But we will live as Red Earth People."

But as the food grew scarcer, others looked upon the White Ones' fields with hunger.

We reached the river of the Raccoon and camped. We remembered well its windings. It was there my brother spoke to Bright Eagle.

"I am strong. I ride the horse brought by my sister from the White Ones. I would sell the horse to White Ones for food and walk to the River Iowa."

My quiet brother had never said so many words before.

Bright Eagle and my uncle, Little Bear, and the other men talked long that night. In the morning, Bright Eagle and my brother led Raccoon-Man's horse toward the White Ones' settlement.

I wanted to say to them, "It was a gift. From my White Ones. If you sell the gift, I have nothing left of

White Gull. Nothing left of Raccoon-Man. They die in me." But I did not speak, for I knew my people had need of food.

When Bright Eagle and my brother returned, they had food for us all. After that Laughing Wind no longer walked beside my brother. Instead she walked with Bold Beaver, who rode a pony.

We were lean and tired and worn—like coyotes in late winter—when we made our last camp, a sun's walk from the River Iowa. We were a weary people hungry for our land.

While others slept, I walked with Bright Eagle down the White Ones' road and sat with him beneath a clump of sumac, now flamed red.

We sat apart. We touched but with our eyes.

"The way ahead is long." He spoke slowly.

"Only one sun separates us from my grandmother."

"I speak of moons and seasons. Not of suns. Our land awaits us. We have no fields. We have no harvest. We have but little seed for planting. And soon the winds and snows will beat about our lodges. Our children will cry with hunger. Our old ones die. We will feast on sorrow and fast on joy."

I heard fear in his voice.

"We will be. . . ," I said, pausing to seek my words, "we will be as seed hidden beneath snows. Each waits to send its roots into the earth. Each waits to claim its place upon the land. So shall we, as seeds, endure."

"You speak wise words," he said and turned his face up to the sky. "Yes. As the river of stars that runs above

us, so are our people. What has been. What is. What will
be. All are one."

"All are one," I said. "The seed. The plant. The
harvest."

"Gray Gull has taught you well. Many times I
heard such words from her. But as you speak, the words
grow strong in me."

"Gray Gull's words are true. Gray Gull's words are
many, but they are true. I learned much from her. Often
with fasting and with ashes on my face. Once my face
was blackened for five suns."

"And I thought you a quiet one. What did you do?"

"I swam with the lazy girls. I often hid from Gray
Gull along Stony Creek when she had work for me. But
Gray Gull was a hunter. She knew my ways."

Bright Eagle nodded. "That is why Bluecoats never
found her. She also knew their ways. Often in her lodge
we spoke of how to hide and where we might stay in
safety."

"Was it hard upon the Iowa while we were in
Kansas?"

"It was easier to starve and be free than to grow fat
and be counted."

"Grow fat!" For the first time, he angered me. I told
him, "When did we grow fat? We planted in fields where
only sand fleas grew. Our people sickened from the night
mists and the pox. Our warriors fought Cheyenne and
Comanche for the buffalo. How could we grow fat?"

Bright Eagle laughed. I had not heard the sound
before. "So, Hidden Doe is not always quiet. That is
good. But I spoke not of you. I spoke of the others who
forget our ways. The ones White Ones call 'Reservation
Indians.' "

I touched the silver and turquoise beads that hung at my throat. "Reservation Indians. The words are ugly. Like others I learned at the White Ones' school. I do not like the sounds."

He turned to look at me. "What sounds would you hear? There are words I would speak to you such as you have never heard. I would breathe them on your skin. I would have them touch your spirit as it quickens in you."

I loved the warmth his words kindled in me.

Bright Eagle spoke again. "It has been long since we first spoke. Longer still since first I saw your eyes. Together we have talked; together we have walked many steps. Each time I see you, each time I hear your voice, you appear to me as if you had never been before. As Grandmother Earth is born anew each planting season, so it is when I am with you."

"But one more sun," I said, so softly I did not think he heard, "and we will lodge along the Iowa."

"It is so. You will build your lodge. Would you have me share it with you?"

"It is good. I will speak your name to my brother," I said, and we rose and walked together back to our camp.

FOURTEEN

We followed the White Ones' road now.

The sun hid behind gray clouds, for we had come to the Moon of the First Freezing. The road was wide and deeply rutted. We could have walked more easily on our own trails, but fences barred our way. The morning chill hung through midday, and I was glad I carried the bearskin on my back.

On other days our morning steps were quick; steps that carried us into evening, slow. This day we kept our morning pace. We did not stop to rest.

On both sides, as far as we could see, were rows of dried corn stalks, set off from us by fences, broken by more fences shutting in the White Ones' lodges. Some lodges were of logs. Others were of naked wood cut smooth, and some were of a white that blinded our eyes.

I walked with Bright Eagle.

"Why do the White Ones work at fences? How can they find wood for burning when they use it all for such?" I asked.

He looked down at me from his pony and then across the field of fences. "I think it is because they are not one. They do not trust each other."

"It is most sad," I said. "They do not learn from us."

It was then we heard the clatter of a White One's wagon on the road behind us. Our people moved aside to let the White One pass, but when he reached Bright Eagle, he stopped.

"You the chief, boy?" he shouted, as he spit a stream of tobacco on the road. "You that bunch of Fox supposed to be comin' up from Kansas?"

"I am no chief. I am Bright Eagle. We are Mesquakie."

"Makes no matter," the White One went on, climbing down from the wagon. "Just thought I'd show you a few nice goods I got here. Trinkets for your squaws. Traps for your men folk. I'll trade for whatever you got. Ponies. Hides. Even carry you on credit. Your government payments should be coming in pretty soon."

The White One thrust his hand into the wagon and pulled out a string of glass beads of many colors. The beads were not strung carefully. They would easily break, I could see.

"Here. Give this to your little squaw. Is that her?" and he held the beads out to me.

I turned away from him, and Bright Eagle moved his pony between us.

"We have no need of these things," Bright Eagle said. I heard the anger in his voice. My uncle, Little Bear, nodded.

"Well, if you're not interested in this, I got something here in the wagon you will like. A fresh batch." He flipped up the corner of the canvas cover.

Many bottles of White Ones' whiskey filled the wagon.

"Want a taste?" he asked, picking up one of the bottles and pulling at the stopper. "It's free. Taste is, anyway," and he chuckled and spat again.

"We do not trade. We move on," Bright Eagle said loudly and urged his pony forward. We followed.

The White One stayed beside his wagon and called after us, "Well, let me know if you change your mind. I'll always be around."

We quickened our steps.

When we were far from the White One's wagon, I looked back. Bold Beaver no longer rode his pony. He walked with Laughing Wind. She wore the glass beads, and they talked in loud and laughing voices.

The road climbed a steep hill, and when we reached the top, we met two white children riding on one horse. The girl, who held the horse's straps, was the age of the White One I had watched on Stony Creek. The boy-child, hugging her waist, was smaller yet.

As we drew near, the boy-child hid his head against her shoulder and began to cry.

"I'm afraid . . . of Indians. I want to go home."

The girl bit into a shiny apple and laughed. "Scardy-cat! They can't hurt us. They're Reservation Indians."

She threw the apple on the ground and trotted past.

I stopped and looked with hunger at the apple. She had taken but one bite. Though I would not have eaten it, I would have saved the seeds. I swallowed hard and kicked the apple into the grass beside the White Ones' road.

I did not speak for many steps, and then I asked Bright Eagle, "How long before we reach our land?"

He pointed. "There where the fences end. Where the mist from the river rests upon the trees. It is a short way now. Soon we will sit in Gray Gull's lodge."

Far down the road, a dark shape moved toward us. As it neared, we saw the horse was old, as was the White One in the buggy. He pulled off the road to make way for us and waited.

When we were almost to him, he called out, "So you made it. Heard you were coming." He looped the driving straps around a pole of the buggy and climbed down.

Bright Eagle guided his pony toward the man. "It is good to meet an old friend again," he said.

The White One walked over to Bright Eagle and held out his hand. Bright Eagle got down from his pony and clasped the hand. Behind us, our people waited.

"Wanted to welcome you and your people back to Iowa. Been keeping an eye out for you folks ever since I found out we'd be neighbors. You look a sight thinner than when you was here before."

My uncle, Little Bear, came to the White One and there was more clasping and shaking of hands.

"It is Quaker Man," Bright Eagle said to us. "He was kind to Gray Gull when winter winds were cruel."

"Name's Anson Cook," the man said, taking my hand and moving it up and down. His hand was rough like tree bark, but warm. His face was bearded white, and I thought of Raccoon-Man.

"Our way was long." Bright Eagle spoke to this man as he would with my father. "But you helped make the path."

"Weren't nothing. Just wrote a letter to the governor down there at Iowa City. Got up a petition. Neighbors signed it. Said we'd all be glad to have Mesquakie back here."

"Your words were good," Bright Eagle said.

"Well," the White One said, "you're almost home now. Ponies look done in, though."

Bright Eagle nodded.

"Well," the White One went on, "they say we're in for a rough winter. It's startin' early. Been pretty chilly for November. I been thinking. Finished my corn-picking today. Ain't got no cattle. If you folks want to use that south field there for your ponies, there's probably enough corn left in the field to keep them all winter. You'd be doin' me a favor. What say?"

Like White Gull, he spoke many words and did not stop to breathe.

"Our ponies would live well," Bright Eagle said.

"Never have felt quite right about the government chasing you out of here a few years back. There's some round here, of course, claim the government's givin' ya handouts. Tain't so. You've a right to them payments. It was your land. You didn't get a fair price for it either." He pushed back his hat and scratched his head. "Well, I best be getting on. And I suppose you folks want to get settled in for the night. I'll be down to call on you. Want to talk about some sugar maples I got up there on the hill. I don't know how to tap 'em."

Bright Eagle said, "We will speak again." All shook hands and we walked on.

"This is our land," Bright Eagle stretched his hand toward the River Iowa.

We stopped and looked across the marshy lowlands, to the quiet river, and upon the wooded hills. There were no fences here. The land was as it had been. We were home.

Bright Eagle led us to a clearing where three wickiups stood. Smoke curled in thin wisps from the largest. Our people came to greet us. My grandmother was not among them.

Our women moved in the winter twilight to seek the wood and branches for the new wickiups. Bright Eagle and my uncle, Little Bear, with my brother and the others sat and talked with Roaring Thunder.

I loosed the straps that held the bearskin. No one spoke Gray Gull's name to me, and I feared to ask of her. I moved down toward the river. I, too, must build a lodge. And as I chose the willow limbs, I thought on Gray Gull and her words when we had parted: "Though I die, I will be here waiting for you."

My branches were cut and bound tightly for carrying. I sat beside our river and watched the mingling of water among the stones.

I felt a hand upon my hair.

I knew the touch. I had not heard her steps. She was a hunter.

"I am here, Hidden Doe," she said.

I turned to look upon her, but she was moving slowly up the path, bent low beneath a load of firewood.

I strapped the willow branches for my lodge upon my back and followed after Gray Gull.

THE BEGINNING

"GET THE BIRTH HOUSE READY!" Gray Gull shouted.

The harvest was ripe. All day I had worked in the field. At midday I told Gray Gull of the first pain.

"The child must not be born in the fields. It will be disgraced," Gray Gull warned.

Not once had I faltered, though I was big with child and the baskets of corn were heavy on my back.

"Put the birth house by the river. For the cleansing."

The women ran quickly from the fields and rushed to the willows while Gray Gull chose the sturdy lodge poles.

"They must be strong. This is her first."

Children played and wrestled on the cooling grass. Dogs barked. At the edge of the clearing, Bright Eagle and the others sat and talked of those still left in Kansas.

The pains were coming faster now.

The old women tugged the willow branches over

the bent lodge poles as Gray Gull fastened the leather straps in place.

"Now blankets," she ordered.

Laughing Wind brought them to her.

"Come to the birth house," Gray Gull said. "Hold to this strap when you feel the pain. I will be outside."

Gray Gull moved to the river bank and sat down in the drying grass. "Grandmother Earth, the time comes round again. All changes like the seasons; all remains the same. Share your wisdom with the girl-child who will be. We have need of strong women."

The pains came. I made no sound.

"Gray Gull," Laughing Wind whispered. "One has come from Kansas. He speaks with Little Bear and the others of words from Great Bear."

"He will speak of good. More of our people come to join us."

Bright Eagle sat beside Little Bear and listened to the messenger. "I bring money from Great Bear. For more land."

Bright Eagle nodded, his eyes shining.

"It is more seed," the one from Great Bear said. "Once the land of the Wisconsin was ours. The land of the Big Water ours. Then all was gone. Now this land is ours again. Soon Great Bear and the others will move their lodges to join you here."

"It is good," Little Bear said.

Dark had come. The village was quiet when Gray Gull entered the birth hut.

"How is the pain?"

"I can bear it," I murmured.
Gray Gull sang:

Come out,
You are a girl.
There is no need to hide in fear.
You are a girl.
Come out.

She sang the song four times.
"Now she will be born. Lie down."
At midnight, the child came.
"The way she slips through the waters of birth, this child shall be free of fear. She will soar above sorrow," Gray Gull proclaimed.

Holding the child in her arms she asked, "What name would you give this girl-child?"

"I would name her . . . White Gull."

So I, Hidden Doe, told it to *my* daughter.

AFTERWORD

THIS STORY IS TRUE. Only the characters are fictional.

The Mesquakie or Red Earth People, sometimes called the Fox, had for many years banded with the Sac, Yellow Earth People, to resist the westward advance of pioneers who wanted land. From 1830 to 1851, through a series of treaties, Iowa was taken over by white settlers. After the Black Hawk War of 1832, the Mesquakies no longer fought, but because they felt the treaties were false, they were still determined to stay upon their Iowa land. In 1845, all Sac and Fox were ordered to move to a reservation in Kansas. When the United States soldiers came to enforce the order, a few Mesquakies managed to stay along the Iowa River.

The Mesquakies believed that people could not own the earth. Yet they understood that to return to Iowa, they would have to adhere to the rules of whites regarding land ownership. They saved their government payments and used them to buy back the same land they had been forced to leave. From 1852 on, the Mesquakies gradually returned, buying more and more land until they owned 3200 acres along the Iowa River, outside the town of Tama. Within a few years, the other tribes who remained on the reservation in Kansas were again uprooted and pushed farther south and west.

Gray Gull, however, understood that there was a problem even greater than loss of land. The United States Government insisted that Native Americans forget their own history, traditions, language, and religious values and accept, instead, the beliefs and customs of the white culture. It was this Mesquakies resisted most.

And so today, the tribe, as a unit, owns the land where Mesquakies live. Gray Gull's words, "We are one. We are Mesquakie," are still true.

ABOUT THE AUTHORS

HADLEY IRWIN is the pen name of Lee Hadley and Annabelle Irwin. Both native Iowans, they teach in the English Department of Iowa State University at Ames and each has authored articles on adolescent literature. They are the co-authors of *The Lilith Summer*, a 1979 Feminist Press book, and *Bring to Boil and Separate*, a 1980 publication from Atheneum.

ABOUT THE FEMINIST PRESS

THE FEMINIST PRESS offers alternatives in education and in literature. Founded in 1970, this nonprofit, tax-exempt educational and publishing organization works to eliminate sexual stereotypes in books and schools, providing instead a new (or neglected) literature with a broader vision of human potential. Our books include reprints of important works by and about women, feminist biographies of women, and nonsexist children's books. Curricular materials, bibliographies, directories, and a newsletter provide information and support for women's studies at every educational level. Our inservice projects help teachers develop new methods to encourage students to become their best and freest selves. Through our publications and projects we can begin to recreate the forgotten history of women and begin to create a more humane and equitable society for the future. For a catalogue of all our publications, please write to The Feminist Press, Box 334, Old Westbury, New York 11568.

This book was made possible by the work of many people, including The Feminist Press staff and other individuals who have an ongoing relationship to the Press: Sue Anger, Jeanne Bracken, Brenda Carter, Ranice Crosby, Sue Davidson, Shirley Frank, Brett Harvey, Florence Howe, Frances Kelley, Emily Lane, Carol Levin, Kam Murrin, Elizabeth Phillips, Karen Raphael, Marilyn Rosenthal, Helen Schrader, Nancy Shea, Nivia Shearer, Anita Steinberg, Susan Trowbridge, Sandy Weinbaum, Sharon Wigutoff, Sophie Zimmerman.

DATE DUE